Firey. Tempestuous. Irresistable?

Go from drab to dazzling in just seven short days. Dr. Dwayne Dudley shows you how to put POW in your personality. THIS BOOK WILL CHANGE YOUR LIFE.

Well.

I didn't know who Dr. Dwayne Dudley was, but I did know that if anyone needed to put POW in her personality it was me. If anyone qualified for "Drab Person of the Year," it was me. I looked at the picture of Doña Veronica on the cover of *Sweet Suffering Love*. Firey, tempestuous, irresistible; a woman who drove that gorgeous, hot-eyed gueriila leader half-mad with passion.

I doubted that Dr. Dudley could make me over into Doña Veronica . . . but perhaps, after seven days, Adam Holmquist might — just maybe — say hello to me in front of my locker.

You have to start somewhere.

point

ELLEN CONFORD

Seven Days to a Brand-New Me

SCHOLASTIC INC.
New York Toronto London Auckland Sydney

ISBN 0-590-43824-7

12 11 10 9 8 7 6 5 4 3   2 3 4 5/9

To Robert Redford: He knows why.

The Day Before Day One

Adam Holmquist
Mrs. Adam Holmquist
Madeline Holmquist
Mrs. Madeline Kemper Holmquist
Maddy Holmquist

THE PHONE RANG. I took the piece of paper on which I'd been testing out my version of the Impossible Dream, crumpled it into a little ball, and tossed it toward the wastebasket.

"Hello?"

"Hi, Maddy, what's happening?"

"Oh," I said dully. "Hi, Sandy."

"Gee, you make a person feel warm all over. Who were you expecting?"

"I was expecting nobody, but I live in hope."

"Well, that's what keeps us going," Sandy said cheerfully. "You doing anything?"

I'm practicing being married to a boy who not only doesn't know I'm alive, but who, if he somehow found out I existed, would say, "So what?"

I sighed.

"Are you doing anything?" Sandy repeated impatiently.

"Sort of, if fantasizing counts."

"You want to do something in real life?" she asked.

"Like what?"

"Like going to the mall. I have to get new sneakers."

Sandy is on the girls' track team and a long-distance runner. She shops for sneakers like the First Lady would shop for her Inaugural Ball gown. She doesn't just walk into the sporting goods store and say, "Size eight, Adidas, blue." She tries on twenty-seven different pairs. She flexes her feet. She jogs in place. She sprints down the aisle of the store in each pair she tries on. She examines seams, soles, innersoles. She ties the laces three different ways. She engages in long, incredibly dull conversations with the salesman. . . . Going sneaker shopping with Sandy is a project only slightly less complicated than launching a space probe of Venus. And infinitely more boring.

But Sandy Spector is my best friend.

Still . . . "Ah, I don't know, Sandy. That could take up the whole afternoon."

"You got something better to do?"

I looked at the crumpled piece of paper on the floor. (I had missed the wastebasket.)

"Only in my imagination," I said. I didn't add that my imagination, in this case, was much more exciting than what she planned to do in "real life." My depression deepened. "Okay, okay, come on over."

* * *

Sandy and I walked to the mall and I left her in the sporting goods store to flex, tie, examine, and sprint to her heart's content. I went two stores down to the paperback bookshop. It could be an hour before she found the Perfect Puma, so I browsed among the titles in the "Historical Romance" section.

All the books had titles like *Passion's Bitter Fruit*, and *The Flame and the Phlox*. All the covers had pictures of bare-shouldered women with masses of red or black hair tumbling over their *extremely* low-cut gowns, gazing with fiery eyes at dark, passionate men with open shirts and tight trousers. You could almost see their chests heaving as they panted at each other.

I picked *Sweet, Suffering Love* off the rack and looked at the blurb on the back. *"She was the daughter of Don Carlo Albeniz and he was a ruthless guerrilla leader, but their passion spanned three continents and two wars."*

That looked promising. I opened the cover to the little excerpt they always print in the front to tantalize you.

"Do not come one step closer," she warned, her eyes blazing. She clutched her cloak around her and brandished the silver dagger.

"I have fought for you, Doña Veronica," Ernesto said savagely. "I have paid for you, I have killed for you, I have suffered two years in a prison hell for you and I will have you. The devil himself could not stop me now."

He ripped the cloak from her shoulders and —

"Maddy?"

"Oh!" I nearly jumped out of my skin. "Sandy, you scared me." I closed the book, my pulse racing like Doña Veronica's must have been — and not just because Sandy had startled me.

"Did you get your sneakers?" I casually tucked the book under my arm.

"Not yet. I need your opinion."

"My opinion on sneakers? Sandy, you know I don't know a thing about sneakers. You're the expert."

"Yeah, but I can't choose between two. I've narrowed it down to two."

"That's a start, anyway," I grumbled. "What do you need me for?"

"Well, all other things being equal, I want you to see which pair looks better on my feet."

"Oh, for heaven's sake. All right, just let me pay for this."

We walked toward the front of the store. Suddenly I stopped short in front of the new nonfiction. There were a whole lot of titles like *Pulling Your Own Wagon* and *How to Be Numero Uno* and *Dress Your Way to the Top*, but right in the middle of the display was a book with a green cover and yellow letters that shrieked out to me:

SEVEN DAYS TO A BRAND-NEW YOU!

"Come *on*," Sandy said. "The guy's waiting for me."

"Hold it a minute." I picked up the book and looked at the smaller print under the title.

Go from drab to dazzling in just seven short days. Dr. Dwayne Dudley shows you how to put POW in your personality. THIS BOOK WILL CHANGE YOUR LIFE.

Well.

I didn't know who Dr. Dwayne Dudley was, but I did know that if anyone needed to put POW in her personality, it was me. If anyone qualified for "Drab Person of the Year," it was me. I looked at the picture of Doña Veronica on the cover of *Sweet, Suffering Love.* Firey, tempestuous, irresistible; a woman who drove that gorgeous, hot-eyed guerrilla leader half-mad with passion.

I doubted that Dr. Dudley could make me over into Doña Veronica. Perhaps, after seven days, Adam Holmquist might not be quite ready to chase me over three continents and spend two years in a prison hell for me, but maybe — just maybe — he would say hello to me in front of my locker.

You have to start somewhere.

I dashed upstairs to my room and shredded open the bag from the bookstore. I held one book in each hand and then sat there for a good three minutes, torn between which one to read first. I was dying to know what happened to Doña Veronica after Ernesto ripped her cloak off, but I was also dying to start turning into the kind of person who drives men to such desperate lengths as cloak-ripping.

I glanced at the table of contents in *Seven Days to a Brand-New You!* It was only seven chapters

5

long, excluding the introduction — much thinner than the saga of Doña Veronica and Ernesto. Each chapter was headed with a day: "Day One: Take Stock of Yourself. Day Two: Picturing Your New Image," etc.

I figured it would only take a little while to read the introduction and "Day One" and if I ever expected my life to change and become one tenth as exciting as Doña Veronica's, I'd better postpone the fantasy for a while and start work on the Real Thing.

What do you want out of life? Money, power, excitement, popularity, romance?

No, no, yes, yes, yes.

I can show you how to get all this — and more!

What more *is* there?

In seven short days, you will be a new person — the person you always dreamed of being, the "YOU" you were meant to be. Why settle for ordinary when you can be EXTRAordinary? Why melt into the background when you can shine like a blazing star and light up your life with the radiance that is the new YOU? What do you want out of life?

Adam Holmquist. Preferably chasing me across three continents (and catching me in every one of them), but I'll settle for "Hello, Maddy."

Why settle? You can have what you want, exactly the way you want it.

Okay, okay, I won't settle. How, how how?

6

Just follow my SEVEN-DAY PLAN carefully, honestly and to the letter. Read each chapter thoroughly; underline, take notes and study the IMPORTANT PRINCIPLES at the end of each section. Follow this program faithfully and in just SEVEN SHORT DAYS a BRAND-NEW YOU will look back at you in the mirror — a successful, exciting, dynamic NEW YOU with the world in the palm of your hand and your life more exciting than you ever dreamed possible.

Oh, Dr. Dudley, you don't know what I dream.

If God created the whole world and everything in it in only seven days, why can't you, who know yourself best, create just one new YOU in seven days?

For one thing, I'm not God.

But Dr. Dudley's prose was almost as exciting as the writing in *Sweet, Suffering Love*, and as I plunged into "Day One" my pulse was racing nearly as fast as it had when Doña Veronica was brandishing her silver dagger.

I would do it. I would create a BRAND-NEW ME. I would change from drab to dazzling, shine with a new radiance, sparkle like vintage champagne, and in just SEVEN SHORT DAYS, drive Adam Holmquist right out of his gourd.

Day One

Take stock of yourself. What kind of a person are you? Observe, for today, how you interact with people. Observe how people react to you. . . .

ADAM HOLMQUIST was new in town. He had just started at Longley in September, and since he was a senior, I might never have run into him if the great, benevolent God of Locker Assignments had not decreed that Adam be given the locker right next to mine.

The first day of school, the first moment I saw him, I knew I was in love. He stood there in front of his locker, tall, lean, blond, tanned — to put it simply, the most gorgeous male creature I had ever seen in my life.

I am very much afraid I drooled.

"Can't seem to get this open," he muttered.

I should have said something like "Having trouble with that lock? Sometimes you have to kick it." I should have gone right over and offered to show him how to kick his locker. I should have said *something*.

But I couldn't. I just stood there and stared. (And drooled.)

Why didn't I say, "Let me help you"? Thinking back on it later, I realized my whole life could have been turned around in that very moment if only I'd had the sense to help him open his locker. But instead, all I said was "Mmmff." It came out like a choked little cry.

And as I stood there, paralyzed, tongue-tied, with my pulse breaking all previous speed records, he got his locker open and turned his back on me . . . possibly forever.

After that first day, Adam virtually ignored me. Oh, he nodded occasionally in the morning, and sometimes he'd even toss off a casual, indifferent "Hi" as he stowed his jacket, but there wasn't the least spark of interest in his eyes. He looked at me (or right through me) as if I were olive green and blended in with the lockers.

Weeks went by. I found out his name (written on a notebook), his grade (a surreptitious glance at his math text), and absolutely nothing else about him, except that he didn't seem to be attached to anyone at Longley. At least, I never saw him with a girl. I kept telling myself that there was hope; if he wasn't going with anyone, he was available, and if he was available, there was a chance for me.

And every time I told myself that, I followed it

with a heavy dose of reality. Like, what would the nearest thing to a Greek god see in me: plain, self-conscious, ordinary, bland Maddy Kemper? He was Fettucine Alfredo and I was macaroni and cheese. He was vintage champagne and I was Gallo Jug Burgundy. He was Shakespeare and I was Harold Robbins.

Reality was depressing, but my dreams became more and more interesting as the days went by. My imagination, which really needed little except Adam to stimulate a good fantasy, seemed to be fired by all those historical romances I gobbled up, and many nights a full-scale, Technicolor production of *Passion's Pirate* played out while I was asleep. (Adam wore an eye patch. My jade green velvet gown was tastefully tattered.) My *day* dreams all started out right in the halls of Longley, and were solidly rooted in the present, and the possible (even though improbable) future. But those glorious nighttime epics were pure Hollywood. Besides, in *them* I was as beautiful as Doña Veronica. Or Serena. Or Lady Ashley. Or whomever I happened to be reading about at the time.

How could real life — *my* real life, which con-sisted of sneaker shopping with Sandy, baby-sitting, snap quizzes in biology, an occasional movie that just reminded me of how unexciting my life was, and reading things like *Sweet, Suffering Love* (which did the same)— match up to what went on in my overheated imagination?

It couldn't. At least, it hadn't so far.

But now, with Dr. Dudley's help, I was going to change all that. In seven days, there would be a brand-new me. Adam would notice me — would look *at* me instead of *through* me — his eyes would glaze over and his voice would get husky and he would discover he was hopelessly in love.

My assignment for the first day of my seven-day plan seemed simple enough. I had taken stock of myself the night before, right after reading the first chapter of *Seven Days to a Brand-New You!*

Taking stock of myself left me so depressed I went to bed early. The fact was, I was drab. Boring. Plain. Shy. I studied myself in the mirror. I told myself to find something positive to focus on. I realized if I was going to turn myself into "dazzling" I couldn't go on fixating about how nothing I was.

Okay. Brown hair. Brown eyes. Not too short, not too tall. Not fat, not skinny. I might as well be describing a sparrow. Skin tone, medium. Not bad except at Certain Times of the Month and just before major tests.

BORING!

Personality? I am kind to children and animals. Self-conscious; particularly around boys. Particularly particularly around one particular boy. I have a quick wit — but not too many people know this because I'm too shy to say many of the things I think, except with Sandy and one or two other friends.

ORDINARY!

Clothes? Appearance? I look pretty much like everybody else, which is okay, because I wouldn't want to look weird or anything, but on the other hand, there is nothing about the way I look to make anyone notice me.

DRAB!

Come on, Maddy, I told myself. One good thing to say about yourself, beside the fact that you never, ever once pulled the wings off a fly.

I scrutinized my face in the mirror. I stood back and surveyed the whole picture. Desperately I searched for something, anything to give me hope, to give me a good start for tomorrow, for the first day of my Seven-Day Plan.

Finally, in despair, I decided that my nose was not horrible.

That's when I went to bed.

But now, this morning, all I had to do was observe myself with other people. That shouldn't be too hard. I really don't have to do anything but act like myself and watch myself acting like myself and see how other people act toward me.

I got to school later than usual because I took so long trying to find something to wear. I was looking for something fashionable, yet distinctive, "in" but not run-of-the-mill; something that made me look less like a sparrow and more like a cardinal.

It wasn't until I'd torn my closet apart and reduced four dresser drawers to shambles that I gave up and concluded I didn't own anything except sparrow plumage.

So when I finally got to school, I dashed up the south stairs and down the hall to my locker panting, perspiring, and as graceful as a moose with a sprained ankle.

I thought Adam would be long gone, as it was so late, but there he was, just slamming his locker door shut.

I slumped against the wall to catch my breath. I knew I looked awful. I even sounded awful, gasping for air that way. I didn't want him to look at me, to see me. For the first time in my life, I hoped I *did* blend in with the lockers, that he would look right through me and walk on to his homeroom.

He turned to face me. He smiled. "We're running late today." He waved his hand carelessly and walked off down the hall.

I whimpered.

I fiddled with my combination lock, kicked my locker, and threw in my jacket. Why *today?* He had actually said four whole words to me — two more than he had ever said before. I mean, a *complete sentence.* I checked my pocket mirror to be sure I looked as awful as I thought.

I did. Red face, moist forehead, my breath quickly steaming up the little mirror.

Observe, Dr. Dudley had ordered. I tried — I really did. The thing was, I didn't know whether to be thrilled that Adam had said, "We're running late today," or miserable because he had seen me looking my very worst.

Maybe that was it! I thought suddenly. Maybe I looked so terrible he felt sorry for me. Maybe that's why he finally said a complete sentence to me.

Oh, why was life so unfair?

Observe how you interact with people.

But I didn't interact, I realized. He actually spoke to me, and I stood there, panting and sweating, and didn't say a word! It was a chance — I mean, even if Adam spoke out of pity, it was still a chance. I could have at least said, "Yes, we sure are," or something zippy like "You better believe it," or ANYTHING.

But I hadn't. I hadn't interacted at all.

Dr. Dudley, I thought grimly, *we have our work cut out for us.*

All morning I observed — without much interest — how I interacted with people. Since all I did was attend three classes, I mostly interacted with teachers, and then only when they called on me. So there wasn't that much to observe. I didn't really care about how I interacted with teachers. Some people said "Hi" to me. I said "Hi" back, but I felt kind of distracted. I was still thinking of what I might have said to Adam.

In Spanish, Terence Malley, who thinks he is a wit, leaned over to me and said, "Did you know that there's this island off the coast of California where fourteen percent of the female seagulls are gay?"

Terence enjoys shocking people, so I tried not to show him that I was shocked (which I was). I gaped at him for a moment, then recovered enough to say, "I'll bet they have trouble getting teaching jobs."

Terence snorted appreciatively. I observed Terence snorting, observed my unusual display of quick thinking, and then went back to hating myself for not thinking quickly enough with Adam.

And that was my morning. All in all, not a whole lot accomplished.

At lunch, I met Sandy and my other friends,

Barbara O'Connell and Karen Lazarus, at our regular table.

They were the only people in the world I was completely comfortable with, and that's probably because we've been friends since the fifth grade. And because we've been friends for so long, the fact that Karen and Barbara are so different from me doesn't seem to matter.

Where I'm moody, Barbara is cheerful and optimistic. While I felt like a drab sparrow, Karen always appears to have just stepped out of the pages of *Glamour*. Sandy's life revolves around the cinder track and I get winded sharpening a pencil.

But it doesn't matter. They care about me, and they listen to me, and I can be myself with them. That's all that counts.

"Hey, Maddy," Barbara said as I sat down with my tray, "the chef recommends the meat loaf."

"Too late," I said, "I got the peanut butter sandwich. I don't trust anything ground or chopped in this place."

"It's really not bad," said Karen. "I think they put a little something special in it. I can't figure out what it is, though."

"See if anyone's missing a sneaker," I suggested.

"Where were you this morning?" asked Sandy. "I didn't see you when I went by your locker."

"I was late. I couldn't find anything to wear."

"You look fine," Barbara said kindly.

"Thanks." I sighed.

"Are you depressed *again*?" Sandy asked.

"What again? *Still*." I paused in my chewing to

observe myself being depressed and to observe my friends observing me being depressed.

This made me more depressed. I would have sighed again, but the peanut butter had glued the roof of my mouth to my tongue.

"You're awfully quiet today," Karen said. "Did something happen this morning?"

I shrugged. I swallowed the glob of peanut butter and mumbled, "He said something to me."

"He *did*?" shrieked Barbara. "What did he say?"

"Shhh!" I had let them drag my secret out of me two weeks ago after a movie, but I didn't want the whole school to know. I was almost sorry now I'd told them, but at the time it was a relief to have friends share my suffering. Actually, it still was. Sandy, Karen, and Barbara really did share my suffering; they almost felt it themselves. They agonized almost as much as I did over Adam's total indifference, only they plotted elaborate schemes to get him to notice me.

This was getting on my nerves. I kept having to threaten them with murder if they went through with any of the nifty little ploys they (Barbara, usually) dreamed up. Like the one where Sandy runs down the hall, bumps into me "accidentally" and sends me stumbling into Adam's arms. Brilliant, right?

"He said, 'We're running late today.' "

I looked around at their expectant faces.

"And?" Karen asked breathlessly.

"And nothing. That's it."

They sat back, dejected.

"Well," Barbara said, "it's something. It's more than he ever said to you before."

"That's true," agreed Karen. "What did you say to him?"

"Nothing."

"Nothing?"

Sandy groaned. "You blew it, Maddy!"

"Thanks a lot! Tell me something I don't know. Not only that, but I looked so horrible I didn't even want him to see me. I mean, that just made it worse. The one time he noticed me I looked like Mrs. Attila the Hun."

"He might not be as hung up on good looks as you are," Sandy pointed out. "He might think a person's personality is what's important."

"Well, fine," I said glumly, "but as far as he knows, my *personality* is Mrs. Attila the Hun. I mean, now, by actual count, we've exchanged ten words, not counting a few 'hi's.' And we haven't even really exchanged them, because I haven't *said* anything."

"I think a whole sentence is progress," Barbara said firmly. "And you didn't blow it forever — just for today. Tomorrow morning, you be sure and say something to *him*. Maddy, you have to *try*. You can't just expect him to know you're interested if you stand around like a lump every time —"

"I don't know why," I broke in, "but you're not making me feel any better."

"Look, you have to sparkle a little," Karen said.

"Me? Sparkle?" I don't sparkle. Adam sparkles. He's the vintage champagne. I'm the Gallo Jug.

"Maybe sparkling is asking too much," Sandy said thoughtfully. "But you could at least *talk*."

"All right, all right, I'll try. I don't know what to say, but I'll try."

"Oh, Maddy, you're so clever, you'll come up with something," Karen said.

"And if you don't," Sandy said drily, "you can at least say hello."

Day Two

Picture your new image. What did you learn about yourself yesterday that you want to change? What is the YOU you want to be?

YOU COULDN'T exactly say that the first day of my Seven-Day Plan to create a BRAND-NEW ME had gotten my improvement program off to a rousing start.

"What did you learn from this, Madeline?" I asked myself.

(They do that a lot on television shows. After twenty-seven minutes of madcap misunderstandings and merry misconceptions, one character always turns to another and says, "We learned something from this." Frequently it is something any seven-year-old already knows. That's show biz.)

What did I learn from this?

Mainly that when Dr. Dudley promised me I could go from drab to dazzling in just seven short days, he was being wildly optimistic.

After only one day I was tempted — but not ready — to give up. There were six more days to go before my life changed completely, and I hadn't given Dr. Dudley a fair trial yet.

Picture your new image.

Let's see. I could come to school in a jade green gown with a rose in my teeth, flash my eyes at Adam Holmquist and say, "Hey, gringo." (Assuming I could say "Hey, gringo" while holding a rose in my teeth.) Only, what worked for Doña Veronica in 1830 might not be exactly appropriate for the dull, mustard-colored halls of Longley High School in the 1980s. If Adam spotted me tangoing toward him in a velvet gown with a rose in my teeth, it was entirely probable that he would turn deathly pale, drop his books, and run, shrieking, down the south stairs.

What is the YOU you want to be?

Actually, I don't want to be me at all. I want to be Doña Veronica. However, that's impossible. Okay, barring the jade green gown and the rose in the teeth, what can I adapt from Doña Veronica's personality to use in creating my new image?

I hadn't gotten too far in *Sweet, Suffering Love* because while I was at school, my mother had found it and was devouring it by the time I came home. She kept saying, "Just let me read one more chapter and I'll give it back to you," and then when she finished that chapter she'd say, "Oh, I can't stop now, just a little while longer."

She burned the carrots while reading pages 85 through 88. (I had only gotten up to page 40; I made a mental note to check out pages 85 through 88 before I went back to where I'd left off.)

But I knew something about Doña Veronica's character. She was fiery, headstrong, tempestuous, tall, auburn-haired, and gorgeous. She drove men to suicide. (And cloak-ripping.) She was the daughter of a Spanish nobleman and had been educated in a convent till she was fifteen. Judging by the outfit she was wearing on the cover, the convent hadn't had much of an effect on her.

I am five foot four, shy, and my father is an accountant. (Strike three.) No one in their right mind would describe me as tempestuous. I may be a raging inferno on the inside, but as far as anyone can tell, I'm an introverted little sparrow.

Another thing Doña Veronica was, was a terrific conversationalist. She could banter with men who had Only One Thing On Their Minds — and by page 40 she'd met three of them — and leave them still weak with desire, but in awe of her sharp tongue and quick wit.

Okay. I have a sharp tongue (my friends call it sarcastic, actually) and a quick wit. I may not show it much, but I do have a sense of humor. So I'm not auburn-haired. So I don't come on tempestuous. If I did, I would probably frighten Adam anyhow. I can build from strength. I can concentrate on the assets I have. Let's start with that.

But somehow, just being witty did not seem to be

enough to drive Adam Holmquist out of his gourd.

Leaving Doña Veronica back in the nineteenth century for the moment, since I did not have the physical equipment, or the setting, or the century, to model myself on her entirely, who else, I asked myself, do I admire?

I didn't even have to think about that one. There are two girls in school whom everyone admires — and they are almost total opposites. The only thing they have in common is that they're both wildly popular and neither of them has sat home watching television on a Saturday night since seventh grade. (There is *nothing* good on television before 11:30 on Saturday night. Why do the network biggies assume that all of North America is out partying every weekend?)

Erin Coughlin is tall, cool, blond, and An Achiever. No one resents her for being perfect. Which she is. Honor Society, pianist, Class President, etc., etc., etc. She absolutely radiates competence and confidence. She's friendly without being gushy or pushy, intelligent without acting superior. She's Perfect Person.

Dede DeLibero is short, black-haired, and a cheerleader. She is the Queen of Cute, the Empress of Adorable. She's unfailingly, exhaustingly lively; she is a tease and a practical joker and has all the second comedy leads in the school plays. Dede doesn't walk — she bounces.

Now, somewhere between those two and Doña Veronica was my image. Or some blend of the three. This was getting interesting. It was like whipping up a new casserole. Let's see: a dash of wit (from Doña Veronica and myself), a cup of confidence (from Erin), and a tablespoon of lively (from Dede). Cook (in an overheated imagination) until done.

And serve (garnished with parsley?) to Adam, on a silver platter.

Bon appétit, Adam!

Picturing the new Me, the Me I was meant to be, I bounced up the stairs (lively) and down the hall. In the midst of my bouncing, I wondered whether I oughtn't be walking tall (as tall as possible, anyhow) and coolly, like Erin, so I shifted from bounce to glide in mid-bounce. I might have looked a little awkward, but nobody noticed. Nobody at all. Adam was not at his locker. Adam was nowhere in sight.

What a letdown. I was all ready to dazzle him with my new (multifaceted) image and he didn't even have the decency to show up to be dazzled.

I sighed deeply, turned my lock, and kicked my locker. I kicked it more savagely than I'd meant to, out of pure frustration, and I nearly broke my toe.

"Yow!" I dropped my books, grabbed my toe, and hopped around on one foot. A couple of people turned to look and to ask me if I was okay. The tears in my eyes gave me away.

"Oooh . . . ," I groaned. I was still holding on to one foot and surveying my books and papers scattered halfway down the hall. I must have looked like a nearsighted stork.

At which moment Adam came up behind me and said, "You hurt yourself?"

ARRGGHH!

Why did Fate do this to me? When the great, benevolent Locker God gave me the locker next to Adam's, why didn't he/she consult with the whimsical God of Bad Timing and say, "Listen, lay off the Kemper kid. She's got enough problems."

Don't I *ever* get a break?

Only in the toe. I put my foot gingerly to the floor as Adam stood there, waiting for me to reply to "You hurt yourself?"

I'd had this moment all planned out so well! I was going to look cheerful, lively, cool, and confident (with maybe just the slightest hint of tempestuous peeping out from under my eyelids) and say something witty and thoroughly enchanting. At which point Adam would open his eyes wide and stammer, "Why — why, Miss Kemper, without your hang-ups you're — you're *beautiful*."

And there he was, and here I was, with a broken toe, scattered books, tears of pain in my eyes, and he had actually said three new words to me and I couldn't think of one word to say back. *Again*.

I'd promised Sandy. I'd promised *myself*. I promised to at least try. I'd even sort of promised Dr. Dudley, who, after all, was doing *his* best to help me out.

Adam was just about to turn away, having gotten no answer to his question. It was my last chance — maybe the only chance I'd ever have again. I HAVE TO SAY *SOMETHING*.

"Did you know," I said brightly, "that there's a certain island off the coast of California where fourteen percent of the female seagulls are gay?"

* * *

24

For the rest of the morning I forgot about concentrating on my new image and divided my time equally between cursing myself and cursing Terence Malley.

How could I have said such a dumb thing? I can't even begin to describe the look on Adam's face because I only caught a glimpse of it before I blushed, panicked, and hopped down the hall, dragging my broken toe behind me. The glimpse was not enough to tell me what he was thinking, but my imagination provided me with a few choice possibilities.

The least horrifying was that he thought I was crazy. Then, in ascending order of awful, there was A: he merely thought I was a silly twerp; B: he thought I was subtly campaigning for Gay Rights; C: he thought — oh, God — I was like the fourteen percent of those seagulls (birds of a feather and all that); or D: (and probably worst of all) he thought I thought *he* was gay.

I wanted to die. How could I have any hope of kindling the flame of love in Adam Holmquist's heart if I couldn't even look him in the eye ever again?

There was no reason to continue with my Seven-Day Plan. There was nothing worth living for anymore. I might as well die. I might as well kill myself.

But first I was going to kill Terence Malley.

I limped into Spanish, having no desire to practice bouncing or gliding even if my toe (probably not broken, just bruised) had allowed it. What was the point? If I bounced and acted lively, it was for Adam. If I glided and acted confident, it was for Adam. The whole point of changing my image was to make Adam like me — or at least notice me. Well, he noticed me all right.

"You're limping," Terence said as I took my seat next to him.

"How observant of you," I said coldly.

"Did you hurt yourself?"

My heart and possibly my toe and definitely my life have all been shattered in the space of two minutes, but that's nothing compared to what I'm going to do to *you*, Terence Malley. Did I hurt myself? If dumb Terence hadn't put that stupid idea about homosexual seagulls into my head, my whole life might have been different.

"You have ruined my life," I snarled.

"What? *Me?*" Terence looked almost proud. He probably never dreamed he could have such a major influence on anyone. "How did I ruin your life?"

"You and your stupid seagulls." I dropped my English and geometry books to the floor with a deliberate thud. I yanked open a notebook so hard that I ripped three pages halfway down. I slung the strap of my canvas bag over the back of the chair and smacked my Spanish book on top of the notebook.

Señora Schacter came into the room and closed the door.

"You're in a bad mood," Terence remarked.

"Your powers of observation continue to amaze me."

"Buenos días, mis estudiantes."

26

"Buenos días, Señora Schacter."

"¿Cómo están Ustedes?"

¿Cómo? Rotten, that's *cómo.* Murderous, suicidal, despairing, depressed . . . and that's just for starters.

"Muy bien, gracias."

Muy bien, my Aunt Tillie.

"You said *what?*" Karen dropped her sandwich into her clam chowder. She didn't even try to fish it out. She just stared at me.

"Please," I muttered. "I feel bad enough."

"Maybe he thought it was funny," said Barbara. The eternal optimist, that's Barbara. "Maybe he thought it was *cute.*"

"Puppies are cute," I said bitterly. "Kittens are cute. There is nothing cute about perverted seagulls."

"What got into you?" Sandy demanded. "Why in the world would you say a thing like that? I mean, all you had to say was 'I hurt my toe.'"

"And then," Barbara said excitedly, "he might have helped you walk to class. You could have leaned on his arm and he might have —"

"Don't," I whimpered. "Don't torture me with what might have been. I said it because I had to say *something* and it was the first thing that popped into my head. I promised you I'd try, remember, Sandy? Didn't you tell me to at least say *something?*"

"Yeah, but not *that.*"

"Dumb, stupid Terence Malley," I muttered. I stabbed my fish stick repeatedly with my fork. I didn't eat it, just stabbed it. I pretended it was Terence Malley.

27

"Look, the thing is," Barabara said, "he noticed you. At least he knows you're alive."

"Sure. He finally knows I'm alive and I wish I were dead."

"Oh, come on, Maddy," Sandy said. "It's not the end of the world. Even if worse comes to worst, and Adam does think you're off the wall and never looks at you again —"

I moaned pitifully.

"— you have your whole life ahead of you. This school is filled with guys."

"That's right," said Karen. "Today is the first day of the rest of your life."

"Oh, please. Next you'll tell me there are plenty of fish in the sea. I don't *want* any of those other fish."

"All right, all right," said Sandy. "So don't give up. Maybe you'll see him this afternoon. Maybe you can explain how you were dazed with pain and you can't remember what you said —"

"That's right," said Karen. "You can plead temporary insanity. Or amnesia."

I shook my head hopelessly. How would Doña Veronica handle this? Or Erin Coughlin? Or Dede DeLibero? The answer came back instantly. They wouldn't have to. They'd never have said anything so stupid in the first place.

"How did I ruin your life?" Terence asked.

He's also in my biology class, though he doesn't sit next to me there. It was just before the second bell and Mrs. Frank hadn't come in yet. Terence was leaning over my desk. He actually looked concerned.

"Come on, tell me. How did I ruin your life?"

I sighed. The urge to dismember Terence had passed somewhere between lunch and seventh period. I realized that it really wasn't his fault that I'd acted stupid. It was my fault. He hadn't held a gun to my head and forced me to repeat his remark about seagulls. Convenient as it might be to make Terence the scapegoat, the blame lay squarely on my own shoulders.

"You didn't," I said dully. "You didn't ruin my life."

"Oh." He seemed almost disappointed.

The second bell rang. Mrs. Frank came into the room, smiled at us, and closed the door behind her.

"Listen," Terence whispered urgently. "Did you know that apart from man the only animal that can get leprosy is the armadillo?"

I lost what little was left of my cool. I hit him in the ribs with my lab manual.

I didn't see Adam at his locker that afternoon. I wasn't surprised. I suspected that from now on, he would do everything he could to make sure he didn't run into the crazy person who hopped on one foot and babbled about the sexual preferences of birds. He might even ask to have his locker changed; I mean, for all he knew I might be dangerous.

I limped home alone and went straight up to my room. I didn't make my usual stop at the refrigerator, even though I hadn't touched my lunch. (Except for stabbing it.)

I wasn't hungry. I might never be hungry again. What was the point of eating? Eating keeps you alive. There was no life left for me.

I lay stretched out on my bed, staring at the ceiling. How stupid I had been to think I could ever be anything like Doña Veronica. Or Erin Coughlin. Or Dede DeLibero. The whole idea was idiotic.

I couldn't change myself in seven days. I couldn't change myself in seven *years*. I am what I am. To Erin, self-confidence and perfection are natural. Dede does not have to remind herself to sparkle and bounce; sparkle and bounce were built into her chromosomes before birth. Doña Veronica never took a crash course in How to Make Men Crazy. She just did what came naturally.

None of these things came naturally to me. What had ever made me think I could learn them?

My stomach rumbled.. Actually, I *was* beginning to feel a twinge of hunger.

I sat up on my bed and stared across the room.

On the other hand, there were probably a lot of people who *had* changed their lives from drab to dazzling. Certainly movie stars were not born movie stars. They had to learn to act, they had to learn how to look gorgeous, they had to be discovered. And what about all those self-made millionaires who were born in the slums and started their climb to the top with patched trousers, thirty-seven dollars in cash, and a Dream?

"You can change," Dr. Dudley had promised.

I went over to the desk and picked up the book. I read again the Important Points of "Day Two."

At first, creating your new image may not come easily. There may be pitfalls along the path to success. You may stumble; you may fall. DO NOT BE DISCOURAGED! Mistakes are not tragedies, they are SUCCESS LESSONS! Analyze where you went wrong and you will learn how to go right. Remember, Rome wasn't built in a day. You have five more days to go before the NEW YOU is in complete control.

And never forget: TODAY IS THE FIRST DAY OF THE REST OF YOUR LIFE!

Maybe Sandy was right, I thought, closing the book. Even if the worst happened, and I never succeeded in driving Adam Holmquist out of his gourd, there must be more to life than Adam Holmquist.

Right off the bat I couldn't think of anything, but that was probably because all of a sudden I realized I was starving.

I started downstairs to the kitchen.

I had five more days to work on creating a BRAND-NEW ME. I ought to keep my strength up.

Day Three

Now that you have an image of the YOU you want to be, take a good long look at yourself in the mirror. Is your outward appearance projecting the inward changes that you are making? When people look at you, will they see the NEW YOU or the same old you they've always seen? Are your clothes appropriate for a DYNAMIC, SUCCESSFUL person, or are they merely serviceable garments that keep you decently covered? And what about the rest of you? Almost anyone can look better than they do, but it takes work. YOU CAN LOOK TERRIFIC IF YOU WANT TO. Analyze yourself. Be painfully honest. Then get to work. Today is the day to start making yourself look like A MILLION DOLLARS!

I HAD TAKEN a good look at myself in the mirror for Day Two and gotten so depressed that I went to bed early. But Dr. Dudley was right. I couldn't find anything in my closet that wasn't merely a "serviceable garment" to keep me "decently

32

covered." My outward appearance was not projecting the New Me.

Of course, I didn't exactly have a clear picture of what the New Me should look like, but wasn't it enough to know that I didn't want to look like the Old Me anymore?

There really wasn't much I could do with my face or my hair. To be honest, my hair is pretty decent — nothing spectacular, you understand, but I have a good, short cut and I wash it and blow-dry it every day, so it usually looks all right. Maybe I could use a little eye makeup or something. . . .

My wardrobe, though, left definite room for improvement.

"Mom?"

She looked up briefly from *Sweet, Suffering Love*. She was about three quarters of the way through it. "Mmm?"

"I need new clothes."

"Me too."

"Mother."

She tore herself away from the nineteenth century reluctantly and put her finger in the book. "Sorry, hon. What did you say?"

"I need new clothes."

"Why? Have you grown?"

"Not physically."

"Oh," she said, as if she understood. "You feel the need for a change."

"I am *desperate* for a change," I groaned. "I own absolutely nothing that doesn't make me look like a big, fat zero."

Her eyes were drawn back to the book. "You're not fat, dear," she said absently.

"That was just an expression, Mom."

"I think you always look very nice."

"Mother," I said urgently, "I don't want to look 'very nice.' I want to look *sensational*."

"I see. Well, just how much will you need to make you look sensational?"

"I don't know. I'm not even sure where to begin," I admitted. "What I really ought to do is toss out everything and start all over."

"You're joking. You bought new school things only two months ago."

But that was before I knew I had to create a BRAND-NEW ME.

"Couldn't you," she said carefully, "just buy one or two new things that would coordinate with what you already have? You know, just perk up your wardrobe with a few clever touches?"

"You sound like a magazine," I grumbled.

She laughed. "Where do you think I got the idea? Look, how about buying a couple of new things and settling for looking sensational part of the time and very nice the rest of the time?"

"Let's talk cold, hard cash," I said. "I have some baby-sitting money saved up. Not a whole lot, but —"

"If this is really important to you —"

"It is, it *is*, Mom."

"Then how about an advance on your birthday present? I could give you part now, but you'll have less then."

"That would be great!" By December 14, the

34

BRAND-NEW ME might have succeeded in snaring good old Adam. Who could ask for a better birthday present than that?

Karen and Sandy agreed to go shopping with me on Day Three. As soon as school was over, we headed straight for Sunset Mall, lugging our books along with us.

"What are you looking for?" Karen asked.

"I don't know," I said helplessly. "Something different. Something exciting. Something that doesn't look like me."

"Something to make Adam notice you," Sandy teased.

"I think you always look very nice," Karen said loyally. "And besides, Adam noticed you yesterday. When you said that about the seagulls."

"Maybe Maddy wants a disguise," Sandy said. "If she looks different enough he won't know it was her."

I stopped short in front of Zingy Things. "Let's just," I said grimly, "never mention those seagulls again, okay, friends?"

"What have you got to work with?" asked Sandy, as we went inside Zingy Things.

"Just my basic body," I said, a little confused.

"I mean, how much money?"

"Oh. Fifty dollars."

Karen looked around. "Well, where do we start?"

The shop was done in silver and black, with rather dim lighting and very loud rock music blaring from some hidden speakers.

A saleswoman approached us. "Can I help you?"

she shouted. "Are you looking for something special?"

"Yes," I shouted back.

"What?"

"Something special," I repeated, louder.

"Yes, but what would that be?"

"I don't know," I yelled, feeling distinctly silly. "I just know it has to be special."

"Oh. Well, maybe you'd better look around. If you find it, I'll be right over here." She pointed vaguely toward the back of the store.

Karen was already flipping through one of the racks. "Hey, how about this?" she called. She pulled out a short, silver dress with shoulder straps as thin as vermicelli. It actually glowed, as if it were made of thousands of teeny light bulbs. Doña Veronica would have loved it if discos had been around in 1830.

"For what?" I cried. "Where am I going to wear that? I need something for *school*."

Karen stuck the dress back on the rack. "Why didn't you say so?"

"Pants," Sandy said. "Or a skirt. Why don't you start from the bottom and build up from there?"

That sounded reasonable.

Sandy picked out a pair of emerald green velvet jeans.

Karen picked out a pair of electric purple satin jeans.

"Are you kidding?" I wailed. "I can't wear those to school."

"You said you wanted something different," Karen pointed out.

36

"You said you wanted something that didn't look like you," Sandy added.

"Yeah, but I don't want to look like Dolly Parton either," I said. "Come on, somewhere between bland and bizarre there's got to be a happy medium."

We pawed through three racks of pants until I found two I'd even try on.

"They don't look all that different from what you usually wear," Sandy said.

"Did you notice the prices?" Karen frowned. "I don't think your fifty dollars is going to go very far."

"There are plenty of other stores in the mall," I said determinedly.

"Are we going to go to every one of them?" asked Sandy.

"If necessary."

At five o'clock we slumped into a booth at Burger Belle.

My faith in Dr. Dudley was definitely shaken.

I don't know how he could have allotted only one day to changing your appearance. Of course, I had to spend most of my day in school, so I actually only had half a day to work on making my outward image dazzling. But even if I'd had a full day, it couldn't have been enough. It had to be easier for a slum kid with patched trousers, thirty-seven dollars, and a Dream to make himself a millionaire than it was for me to make myself look like a million dollars in half a day on fifty bucks.

"I'm exhausted," Karen moaned. "And my arms are killing me. We should have stuck our books in one of those lockers."

Sandy contemplated the shiny list of "Burger Belle's Bounty" over the counter. "I'm starved. I think I could eat three Hacienda Burgers. Or maybe two Hacienda Burgers and a Chili Dog. Or maybe one Chili Dog, one Hacienda Burger and one Hickory Dickory Taco. What are you going to have, Maddy?"

"How can you think of food at a time like this?" I wailed. "We've been to six stores and all I've gotten is one pair of jeans. And I got them at the first place we tried. And you're right — they don't look all that different from what I've already got at home."

"But they did look great on you," Karen said. She rubbed the insides of her elbows. "Boy, do my arms hurt."

"What are you going to have, Karen?" Sandy asked.

"I guess a Chili Dog and a Taco."

"Can't you two think of anything else but food? What am I going to do? We've been shopping for two hours and all I've got to show for it is one dumb pair of pants."

"Well, we have to eat to keep our strength up," Sandy said. "At the rate you're going, we'll be here till the mall closes."

"It's hopeless," I sighed. "I'm just not going to change my entire appearance with fifty dollars."

"But, Maddy," Sandy said, "You won't even look at anything really wild. Even if you had two hundred dollars, what good would it do if you don't want to be a little daring?"

38

"I want to be a *little* daring," I said. "I just don't want to be utterly reckless."

"Nobody's going to accuse you of being utterly reckless in gray jeans," Sandy said sarcastically.

"I think they're beautiful," Karen protested. "They fit perfectly and they're such a pretty, soft gray; just the color of a beautiful dove."

Was it progress, I wondered, to go from looking like a sparrow to looking like a dove?

Not when you dreamed of looking like a peacock.

Karen and Sandy went to the counter to get the food.

Sandy was right. I didn't have the nerve to make any really drastic changes in my appearance, even though I was bored stiff with the Old Me. It was hopeless. So what if I found Exactly the Right Shirt and the Perfect Sweater to wear with my new pants? I would hardly look the least bit different from the way I looked every day. Which meant that Adam would not notice me any more than he ever had.

But there's more to life than Adam, I reminded myself.

What more? I certainly wasn't trying to change my image for Sandy or Karen or Barbara.

Sandy and Karen came back with the food.

"Listen, Maddy," Karen said, "you know what? I think instead of concentrating so much on clothes, you ought to fool around with your face."

"I beg your pardon?"

"I mean, your clothes are really perfectly okay. And you're awfully tense about getting anything that looks spectacular —"

"I'd *love* to get something that looks spectacular, I just don't want to make a spectacle of myself."

"Right, right, that's what I mean. So why don't we get you some new lipstick, some stuff for your eyes — I'm pretty good with makeup, and you've got enough money left, even if you get a sweater to go with the pants, and we can go to my house and fool around and give you a whole new face."

"You think it would make a difference?" I asked hopefully. "I mean, you really think I could look sensational with the right makeup?"

Karen seemed slightly uncomfortable.

"Let me rephrase that," I said sourly. "You think I could look *better* with the right makeup?"

Karen brightened. "Sure you could! Much better! Worlds better. Even the plainest person —"

I pushed my Chili Dog away.

Karen looked stricken. "Oh, Mad, I didn't mean you were plain. I just meant —"

"I know what you meant."

"No you don't!" Karen cried. "You have a great face. I mean, really good bone structure and everything."

"I do?"

"Yes, you do! All I meant was that even ugly people can improve their looks if they know how, and you're not ugly."

"Just plain," I muttered.

"*NO!* You've got all the basic equipment you need —"

"Two eyes, one nose, one mouth —"

"*Maddy!* All I'm saying is you could do more with yourself makeupwise —"

"Makeupwise?" Sandy broke in.

"And I can show you how. I study *Glamour* and *Vogue* from cover to cover every month."

"No wonder you're failing geometry and biology," said Sandy.

"Oh, be quiet!" I snapped. "I don't need help in geometry and biology. I need help in glamour and vogue."

In a mere hour and a half we found a sweater to go with my slacks and a bunch of cosmetics that Karen said were the absolute minimum she needed to create my new face.

We walked back to Karen's, leaving Sandy off at her house. She had homework to do and didn't care to stand around and watch Karen change me from drab to dazzling. (Sandy doesn't wear any makeup herself.)

Karen sat me down with my back to her dresser mirror and went to work. It took her about fifteen minutes to get the effect she wanted. She put stuff on my eyes, my cheeks, and my lips. She nearly pulled out my eyelashes with a curler thing that looked like a pair of cuticle scissors with an overbite.

Finally she stood back a little, folded her arms and surveyed her work.

She smiled triumphantly. "Viola!" she cried. "You can look now."

"Don't you mean *'Voilà'*?" I asked nervously.

"Whatever. Look in the mirror!"

I turned around slowly, almost afraid of what I was going to see. Even as I turned I feared A: Karen had overdone the makeup and made me look grotesque, or B: she had underdone it and I didn't look any different.

"Karen!" I leaned forward and stared at myself. "Karen, what did you do? How did you do it?"

"You like it? Don't you look great? Didn't I do a great job?"

"I can't believe it." Neither Fear A or Fear B had come true. I looked different, but not so different that you wouldn't know it was me. I certainly didn't look like Dolly Parton. Karen had done something with my eyelids to make them look sort of smoky and romantic. I lowered them a little and fluttered my lashes. Doña Veronica had eyes like that! There was some color high on my cheekbones that gave my face a little sparkle and excitement and seemed to make those smoky eyes even more dramatic.

"You don't think the lipstick's a little dark?" I asked doubtfully. It was a good bit darker than what I was used to.

"Oh, no, Maddy. Not everyone can wear it, but it's absolutely *the* shade of the season, and with your coloring it would be criminal not to use it."

"If you're sure —"

"I'm sure," she said firmly.

"Oh, Karen," I sighed, staring at myself. "I don't know how you did it."

She smiled smugly. "I told you, Mad. You had all the basic equipment. If you didn't have such great basics to begin with I *couldn't* have done it."

"But *I* don't know how to do it," I realized.

"You will," she said. "Go wash it all off."

"What?"

"Go wash it all off. I'm going to teach you how, step by step."

"Karen, it's late. That could take hours."

"Don't be silly, it won't take hours. You know how to put on most of this stuff already anyhow. I'm just going to show you the subtleties — you know, like the secrets of the Great Hollywood Makeup Artists. Now, go wash your face!"

Day Four

Today is the day you PUT IT ALL TOGETHER. Today is the day you go out in the world for the first time as the BRAND-NEW YOU! Maybe you feel a little nervous about being the NEW YOU. That is perfectly natural. You haven't had any experience being the YOU you want to be. After all, you haven't been BRAND NEW since the day you were born. Today is the day you will be BORN AGAIN. Today you will project the image you have perfected. You will ACT AS IF you have always been a DYNAMIC, SUCCESSFUL person. At first this may seem strange and artificial to you, but in a shorter time than you believe possible, you will no longer be ACTING AS IF you were SUCCESSFUL and DYNAMIC, you will be SUCCESSFUL and DYNAMIC!

I GOT UP fifteen minutes earlier than usual to allow myself time to put on my new makeup, wash it off if I loused it up, and put it on again. It didn't turn out to be as hard as I thought, except for curling my eyelashes with that metal thing. I didn't quite have the hang of that yet. But the eye crayons and pencil were fairly simple, especially since Karen had told me I was supposed to smudge my lids a little with my finger, so if I slipped with the pencil it was no big deal. The trick with the "Peachy Cheek Gleamer" was to smile really wide, so your cheeks went up and out, and then put the stuff on at the highest point and blend it back toward your ears. Naturally, I already knew how to apply the "Moist Mulberries LipSlick."

I stood back and surveyed myself in the mirror. I was wearing my new gray jeans and the gray, black, and white fuzzy sweater I had bought to go with them. The sweater had a little white organdy and lace collar that framed my new face rather nicely.

I smiled at my reflection. I did look different; in fact, I looked pretty good for me. In fact, to be perfectly honest, I looked pretty good, period.

Maybe the lipstick was a bit too dark. . . . No, I told myself firmly, it's just that you're not used to it.

I practiced smiling at the mirror. I would smile this way at Adam today. I lowered my eyelashes and looked out from under my smoky eyelids, the way Doña Veronica looked at Ernesto. (And every other male over the age of fifteen.)

It looked more like a nearsighted squint than a sexy gaze; I decided it needed work.

I smiled some more. I leaned forward to get a good close-up look. I had smudges of "Moist Mulberries" on my front teeth. Hastily I wiped them off with my fingers and went downstairs to breakfast.

My father and mother were already at the table,

drinking coffee and engrossed in separate sections of the morning paper.

My mother looked up and smiled broadly. "You're wearing your new clothes," she said. "Honey, you look marvelous."

"Thank you."

"You look different," my father said, scrutinizing my face. "What's different?"

"You're not listening," I teased. "My whole outfit is different."

He shook his head. "No, it's not the clothes." He sounded puzzled. "You look — I don't know, healthier."

Thank you, "Peachy Cheek Gleamer."

"And that lipstick," he went on. "Isn't that kind of dark?"

I wouldn't let my confidence be shaken. After all, what did my father know about lipstick?

"She has the coloring for it," my mother said. "You're just not used to it."

Neither was I, but Karen had been right about everything else, and if I was really determined to be the Brand-new Me, I couldn't turn cowardly over a little thing like dark purple lips.

There was one small hitch, however, which I thought about all the way to school. Despite what Dr. Dudley thought, I had not firmly established the new image I wanted to project. On Day Two I had tried to be some sort of a combination of Erin Coughlin, Dede DeLibero, and Doña Veronica, and ended up with a mishmash of conflicting personalities, none of which were mine, and all of which actually clashed with each other.

46

I mean, I didn't even know whether to glide or bounce; I didn't know whether to act bubbly or cool; I didn't know if I wanted to be competent or madcap or downright sexy.

I was supposed to have a clear picture in my mind of the kind of Me I wanted to be, and spend today ACTING AS IF I were that kind of person, but here I was halfway to school and I was nowhere near having my act together.

All right, I thought at last. I can't be Erin. I can't be Dede. And I certainly can't be Doña Veronica. Even trying to pick out their best qualities and copying them had confused me, so that wouldn't work. What if I just projected a stronger image of myself? Turned up my volume a little, you might say. After all, I'm not such a terrible person. My biggest problems are shyness, lack of confidence, and feeling plain — but today I don't feel plain. I feel like I'm actually verging on pretty. And that should give me confidence.

That's it, I decided. I'll walk the way I normally walk, without worrying about bouncing or gliding — just hold my head high and walk like a *confident* person.

I will talk like a confident person. I'll even talk to Adam first and not wait helplessly for him to say something to me. I'll ACT AS IF I expect him to *want* to talk to me.

I will positively radiate confidence and wit and charm. Wit I've already got — and I'll just do my darnedest to fake confidence and charm.

* * *

I walked confidently up the south stairs and down the hall to my locker. My heart was pounding, but my head was high.

Adam wasn't there. He hadn't been there yesterday at all; I hadn't seen him since I'd slipped him that choice bit of gossip about the seagulls.

Maybe he *had* asked to change his locker. Or maybe he was just never going to use it again. Or maybe he was sick — or he'd suddenly had to leave town and I'd never get the chance to —

He was coming down the hall! He was looking directly at me as he walked toward our lockers. Hastily I turned and began to fiddle with my lock.

I pulled my foot back to kick my locker, then thought better of it. I wiped my front teeth surreptitiously, just in case they had "Moist Mulberries" stains on them.

Confident, I told myself. Charming. Witty.

He was almost there.

I can't do it. My heart is pounding so hard he'll hear it. I can't say anything. I can't be witty. I can't be charming. I can't be confident. I CAN'T SAY A WORD.

All six-foot blond gorgeousness of him was practically right next to me now.

What made me think I could overcome fifteen years of shyness in one day? My palms are getting sweaty. My tongue is tied in a granny knot. My lipstick is too dark. He's going to wonder why I have purple lips. And teeth.

He is looking right at me. I can feel him looking at me.

IT'S NOW OR NEVER, MADELINE KEMPER. GET HOLD OF YOURSELF!

Adam bent to open his locker.

At least, I thought, at the very least, I can smile at him. I leaned back against my locker and tilted my head to one side. I swallowed several times. This was the way Doña Veronica leaned against wrought iron balconies, flirting from behind a black lace fan. (It was a miracle she never fell backwards off any of them and plunged to her death.)

FORGET DOÑA VERONICA! Adam had his locker open and was hanging up his jacket. *At least smile.*

I took a deep breath. And smiled.

Adam closed his locker. He saw me. He smiled back, tentatively.

"Hi," he said.

"Hi," I said softly. It was a good thing I had the locker to lean on. The nearness of him, the little smile, the "hi," the general Greek godliness of Adam Holmquist was rendering my legs inoperative.

He had his books in his hand. His locker was closed. He was ready to go to his homeroom.

But he didn't.

He was lingering He. was lingering at his locker! He was looking at me.

He lingered . . . at his locker . . . and that's how we met. . . . He looked at my lips . . . which with berries were wet. . . .

A great song possibility, I thought wildly. One of the great love songs.

GET HOLD OF YOURSELF!

I was still wearing my jacket and holding my books across my chest. I realized Adam hadn't even seen my new clothes, but I didn't want to turn my back on him to open my locker and put my stuff away.

I kept smiling. My mouth was getting tired. I began to feel self-conscious. Neither of us said anything; we just kept looking. I didn't want to look away — that would have been the old, shy Maddy. The New Maddy was confident, charming, etc.

Adam cleared his throat.

"Uh, you know, that was really interesting, what you told me about those seagulls."

My jaw dropped. Along with my Spanish book and my biology lab manual.

He reached down quickly and picked them up. He handed them to me.

"Thank you," I whispered.

"Is it — uh — true? I mean, was there a scientific study or something?"

This can't be happening. I swallowed again and tried frantically to project confidence and charm.

With a great struggle, I made my voice bright and cheerful.

"If you think that's interesting," I said, much louder than I'd intended, "you might want to know that besides humans, the only animal that can get leprosy is the armadillo."

Three people who happened to be passing us turned to stare.

My heart sank. My face grew hot; I had the feeling that at this particular moment, "Peachy

Cheek Gleamer" was totally unnecessary. My cheeks were plenty red without it.

Why do I *do* these things? Why do I *say* these things? Isn't it better to say nothing than to sound weird?

Maybe not.

"Really?" asked Adam. "I didn't know that."

Of course he didn't know that. Why should he know that? Surely a person could go through his entire existence without ever knowing that armadillos get leprosy, and still live a rich, full life.

The first bell rang.

"I — uh — better get my stuff away," I stammered.

I opened my locker and threw in my jacket and the books I wouldn't need till after lunch. I closed my locker.

"Well," Adam said.

Say something, Madeline. Say something before he leaves that will keep him interested. Unbelievable as it seems, he does not think you are crazy despite your babbling about armadillos and seagulls.

"Well," I said weakly, "see you." Oh, Maddy, I thought, was that your best shot? Now that I'd run out of seagull and armadillo lore, I guess it was.

"See you."

I smiled as dazzlingly as I could manage, then turned and walked confidently — sort of — toward my homeroom.

Somewhere between first and third period it hit me. Adam was shy. Possibly even as shy as I was. I

51

never saw him talk to anyone at his locker, I never saw him walking with anyone, and he was new in town. Maybe he was having trouble making friends.

It was hard to believe that someone who looked like Adam didn't have girls phoning him around the clock, but maybe he had an unlisted number.

Maybe he didn't think my tidbit about our flaky feathered friends was interesting, and maybe he didn't have the slightest desire to establish a leper colony for armadillos; maybe he was just glad to have someone — anyone — say something — anything — to him!

He obviously didn't think I was crazy. In fact, he seemed grateful that I had talked to him. In fact, if I wasn't imagining it, he wanted me to talk some more.

It was unbelievable. It was incredible. It was too good to be true. But there it was. The divine Adam Holmquist actually wanted to talk to mere, mortal Madeline.

Ah, I reminded myself, but I'm no mere Madeline any more. I am the NEW Madeline. Dr. Dudley was right. I dazzled Adam with my new face, my enticing smile, my quick wit, my calm self-confidence. . . . Well, maybe two of the above.

I slid into my seat next to Terence Malley in Spanish. I beamed at him. By this time I was actually feeling grateful to Terence. I was very glad I hadn't murdered him two days ago. In fact, he could become a very valuable natural resource.

"You look different," he said, studying my face.

Wow, even Terence notices the new me!

"I think it's the lipstick," he went on. "It's so *dark*."

I had been reapplying fresh coats of "Moist Mulberries" between classes, in order to keep my lips looking kissably glossy throughout the morning. (I wanted to be prepared for any emergency.)

I scowled. "It happens to be the 'in' shade this season."

"In the shade maybe it looks better. Ho ho."

"Ho ho," I said sourly. Well, what did I care what Terence Malley thought of my lipstick? Adam certainly must have liked it.

I remembered that I was grateful to Terence. I stopped scowling.

"Don't you," I asked sweetly, "have any more interesting facts to lay on me?"

Terence brightened. "Oh, yeah. Listen, did you know that eighty-four percent of all people who swing have beige drapes?"

I stared at him. I thought that over for a minute. I realized immediately that I didn't want to use this one — especially not now that I suspected Adam was shy — but it intrigued me.

"We have beige drapes," I said thoughtfully.

Terence leered at me.

"Wait a minute, wait a minute," I said, "half the people I know have beige drapes. Beige drapes are very common. I'll bet eighty-four percent of *everybody* has beige drapes."

Terence frowned. "We have gold drapes."

"Listen, haven't you any little goodies that don't deal with sex or leprosy?"

Terence squeezed his eyes shut, as if he were racking his brain. His whole forehead wrinkled. "Well," he said finally, "men with hair on their chests are less likely to get cirrhosis of the liver than bare-chested men."

The bell rang. Señora Schacter came in and closed the door.

And a good thing it was too. I was just beginning to imagine Adam's chest.

"Buenos días, mis estudiantes."

I couldn't get Adam's chest out of my mind.

"Buenos días, Señora Schacter."

Adam's *shirtless* chest.

Terence leaned over and whispered, "Was that the kind of thing you wanted?"

I gulped. I felt like I needed to fan myself with my notebook.

"You have no idea," I murmured.

"Your eyes are like fire," Ernesto panted. *"They burn through my body like branding irons."*

"You are a savage!" spat Doña Veronica, struggling to free herself from his iron grip.

"It is you who make me so, mi querida," he murmured. He grasped her to his heaving chest and seared her lips with blazing kisses.

They use a lot of fire images in these novels. My English teacher would be pleased I noticed that. I didn't linger long over the thought. My own chest was heaving pretty well by this point.

Struggling desperately, Doña Veronica wrenched herself free. There was a sound of ripping cloth and she gasped as her gown tore, baring one creamy shoulder.

Doña Veronica must have had entire trunkfuls of ripped clothes stashed away in a cellar somewhere. Goodwill would have loved her.

"Do not fight me so, my little wildcat," Ernesto breathed. "Your passion speaks far louder than your words."
He strode toward her. She turned to run, but he was too quick, and in an instant she was in his arms again. He smothered her bare shoulder with burning kisses.

(More fire images.)

Her body went limp in his arms. With a deep sigh of defeat, Doña Veronica stopped struggling, and gave herself up to the passion that overwhelmed her. . . .

And about time, too, I thought.
Reluctantly I closed the book and turned off my light. It was late, and I'd been curled up on my bed with Doña Veronica and Ernesto for almost a hundred steamy pages. (When I got to pages 85 through 88, I understood why my mother had burned the carrots. The section fairly sizzled with fire images.)

55

To my great disappointment, I hadn't seen Adam this afternoon.

And things had gone so beautifully this morning. He seemed to be glad to have someone to talk to, even if only about armadillos. If he was shy and lonely as I thought, why didn't he make it a point to come back to his locker in the afternoon to see me again?

Maybe he'd gotten sick during the day and gone home. Maybe he stayed after school for some activity or sport or something. There were a dozen perfectly reasonable explanations for why I hadn't seen him this afternoon — and at least half of them did not involve me.

I'd made a very good start projecting my new image and I was not going to let Adam's mysterious afternoon absence discourage me. After all, it wasn't just today that he hadn't shown up at three o'clock. I realized that while I always saw him at our lockers in the morning, he was not dependable in the afternoons. It could be that his last class was near his locker and his homeroom wasn't, so that sometimes he got all his stuff right after class and left school straight from his homeroom.

Well, tomorrow was another day. Day Five of my Seven-Day Plan. I could take satisfaction in what I had accomplished today. After all, in just four short days Adam had not only noticed me, he had smiled at me, started a conversation himself, and actually seemed to be willing to listen to any freaky facts I wanted to lay on him.

Not bad progress after two months of blending in with the lockers.

I closed my eyes and pictured Adam's chest. I didn't know what it looked like but I enjoyed imagining it. I drifted pleasantly off to sleep. . . .

And dreamt: Adam was the son of a rich rancher, but he lived a double life as a highwayman. I'm not sure why he did this, but he had a good reason. He held up stagecoaches. I was on one of the stagecoaches he held up. He took the money bags, a small iron trunk filled with jewels, and me. (He let everyone else go.) He pulled me onto his horse and rode off with me into the sunrise. (He was only a highwayman at night.)

He wore black. His belt was hammered silver. His horse was a golden palomino. (It matched his hair.)

My shoulders were incredibly creamy. . . .

Day Five

Today is the day you take Life by the scruff of the neck and shake it till it coughs up what you want! The New YOU is ready to go out and grab the brass ring! It's there. It's waiting for you. You worked hard to become the New YOU and you deserve to get what you want. Never doubt for a moment that you are going to get it. Maintain a POSITIVE ATTITUDE. Keep your confidence high and leave your doubts at home. Be sure you're going to get what you want, and you're sure to get it! Money? Power? Romance? Popularity? They're all out there, just waiting for you to stake your claim to them. Set your goal and GET IT!

I REREAD chapter five twice and gave myself a booster shot by reading the IMPORTANT PRINCIPLES at the end of the section before I left for school. Dr. Dudley was a trifle vague about just how to go about grabbing Life by the scruff of the neck. Mostly he said you had to ACT AS IF you already had what you wanted.

In other words, if you wanted a lot of money, you had to start thinking and acting like you already had a lot of money. You had to condition your mind to having money — or whatever your goal was.

My goal — the whole reason, in fact, that I'd embarked on the Seven-Day Plan — was to drive Adam Holmquist out of his gourd. How, I wondered, do I act as if I'd *already* driven Adam out of his gourd?

Most of chapter five dealt with acting as if you had money or power or success. Dr. Dudley didn't dwell very long on love and romance. Actually, all he said was:

Have confidence in your desirability and appeal. Know that you are a worthy object of affection. Radiate that confidence and love-ability wherever you go!

Well, that was fine but what Dr. Dudley didn't tell me was how to acquire that kind of confidence in my love-ability. I had no previous experience on which to build. I'd never gone out with a boy, never been asked out by a boy, never been kissed. Well, once, actually, but that was in the fourth grade and Howie Schroeder did it on a dare. How did I know I had any desirability? As far as I knew, I didn't.

But that was the Old Me. It didn't matter that the Old Me had never driven a boy out of his gourd. This was a whole new ball game — with a New, Improved Madeline Kemper ready to go out there and grab Life by the scruff of the neck.

It would be a nice change. Usually Life grabbed me by the scruff of the neck.

I did have something to build on, I told myself as I walked to school. I had yesterday. All I had to do was ACT AS IF Adam's apparent interest in seagulls and armadillos was really just a cover-up for his interest in me. I would ACT AS IF I knew he liked me, and — *viola,* as Karen would say — before he knew it, he *would* like me. I wasn't sure how that worked, but Dr. Dudley seemed pretty certain about it, and he was a *doctor.*

When you've been walking around with self-doubts for years, it is not easy to "leave your doubts at home," but I tried. I even pictured my doubts piled up on my desk: gray, gloppy things they were, sort of like small, slimy thunderclouds. I pictured ᵗhis pile of doubts, so huge it squished up against the ceiling of my room, with such vividness that I began to wonder how long it would take me to clean the glop off my desk when I got home.

Okay. My doubts were at home on my desk, my confidence was in my side pocket, I had Life by the scruff of the neck, and in a moment, Adam would be in the palm of my hand.

Only, Adam didn't seem to know the game plan for my whole new ball game. He was not at his locker.

My heart sank. I put my jacket away and closed my locker door with a sigh. Maybe he wasn't coming to school today. Maybe he'd already gotten here and gone to his homeroom. Maybe he was late.

I decided to wait awhile. I leaned against my locker and pretended to study my Spanish notes. I looked up frequently to see if Adam was coming. I gave out a few half-hearted "hi's" to people I knew.

The first bell rang. If Adam did come now, there would be only three minutes to convince him of my desirability. Even Doña Veronica needed more than three minutes. (Well, maybe Doña Veronica didn't, but look what she had to work with. You can do an awful lot in three minutes with auburn tresses and a black lace fan.)

I closed my notebook with a sigh of resignation. I started down the hall to my homeroom and suddenly, rounding the corner and walking toward me, there he was.

For one, brief shining moment, my heart soared, my face lit up, my pulse raced . . . and then, *bam*. Thud. All abnormal bodily functions ceased. In fact, all normal bodily functions seemed to grind to a halt.

The Incredible Hunk was not alone.

Mary Louise Dryden was walking next to him, gazing up at Adam's face with a look of absolute and utter concentration, as if she were fascinated by whatever he was saying.

He didn't seem to be saying *anything*, but then, just looking at his face was fascinating enough, wasn't it?

She said something to him. He nodded. Probably agreeing on the date for their wedding, I thought bitterly.

Our paths were just about to cross. Adam saw me. He managed to tear his eyes away from Mary Louise for an instant.

"Hi," he said.

Mary Louise glanced vaguely in my direction. "Oh, hi there," she said.
They walked past me.
Somehow I found my way to my homeroom.

Mary Louise Dryden, for crying out loud. The thought tormented me all morning.

I had started my Seven-Day Plan too late. Mary Louise was a senior. They probably had classes together, or were in the same homeroom and she'd been working on him since the beginning of school. I'd never seen them together before, but then, how often did I see Adam at all? For all I knew, they'd been hanging on each other's every word since the second day of school.

But maybe not. I tortured myself with the idea that Mary Louise had begun her campaign to win Adam two weeks ago, and had just hit her peak today — the very day I was to Act As If *my* campaign had been successful.

I'd had my chances, and I'd blown every one of them. If I'd talked to Adam sooner . . . if I'd found Dr. Dudley's book sooner . . . if, if, if.

All those "ifs" were bad enough, but even more tormenting, more mystifying, more confidence-shattering was the *Why?* Of all the people in Longley Adam could have chosen, why in the world would he pick Mary Louise Dryden?

"Mary Louise Dryden?" Karen said increduously. It was at least the third time she'd repeated it. "Mary Louise Dryden, for Pete's sake?"

"If you say that name one more time," I threatened, "I won't be responsible for my actions."

"But Mar —" Karen stopped herself as I tried to glare at her. It wasn't easy with my eyes full of tears. "I mean, *her*," she said. "She's so — I mean, she's not — I mean —"

"You mean, even *I* look good next to Mary Louise Dryden," I said miserably.

"You told me not to say her name again," Karen pointed out.

"Well, I'm allowed," I replied unreasonably. "I'm the one that's suffering."

"Oh, Maddy," Sandy said, "you suffer at the drop of a hat. You're leaping to the most incredible conclusions."

"He couldn't take his eyes off her," I moaned. "You should have seen them, you'd believe me. She's enchanted him. *Entranced* him. Put a spell on him."

"Mary Louise Dryden?" Sandy laughed.

I turned on her savagely. *"I warned you!"*

"All right, all right, I'm sorry. But it's — bizarre. Mar — I mean *she* couldn't enchant a gnat."

"Maybe she has a nice personality," Barbara suggested.

"She has the *personality* of a gnat," I said.

"Then how do you explain it?" Barbara asked. "She has no personality, she's not pretty —"

"Not pretty!" I cried. "She has a body like a stick, a face like vanilla pudding, she gets her clothes from —"

"Maddy," Sandy said, "you're raving. Get hold of yourself."

I slumped over my tray.

Karen pulled it away. "You're getting mashed potatoes in your hair," she said.

"Who cares? Who cares?"

"Look, this is crazy," said Barbara. "If she has no looks, no charm, no personality, how could Adam possibly be interested in her?"

"I don't know," I whimpered. "Don't you think I've been trying to figure it out all morning? It's driving me crazy."

"Maybe she has that certain spark, that indefinable quality, that *Genie says kwoy*," Karen said. She sounded as if she were quoting *Glamour*. She probably was.

"I think you mean *je ne sais quoi*," Sandy said.

"Whatever." Karen shrugged. "Maybe she's got it."

"But what is it?" I pleaded. "And where is she hiding it? And how do you get it?"

"Maddy, will you please lower your voice?" Sandy said. "People are staring at us."

"Let them stare." Who cares? Who cares about anything?

"And I still think you're being ridiculous," Sandy went on. "You have absolutely no evidence that Adam likes her. They just happened to be walking down the hall together —"

"Drooling at each other," I muttered.

"Now you *are* exaggerating," Sandy said.

"He's shy," I said dully. "She came on to him. Just when he was feeling friendless and alone and vulnerable she went in for the kill."

"It doesn't make any sense," Barbara objected.

"He's so cute someone else besides Mary Louise must have come on to him by now. I'm with Sandy. I think they were just walking down the hall together and you're jumping to conclusions."

The bell rang.

"Maddy, you didn't eat a thing," Karen said worriedly.

I just shook my head. I had no appetite. No appetite for food, no appetite for life, no appetite for trying to unravel the mystery of Adam and Mary Louise. I certainly had no appetite for any more self-improvement schemes. If someone like Mary Louise Dryden could drive Adam Holmquist out of his gourd, Dr. Dudley could throw his list of IMPORTANT PRINCIPLES right out the window. And throw himself out after them.

I walked through the rest of the day in a fog. I really didn't have the vaguest idea of what was going on around me. Terence said something to me in biology about the mating habits of the two-toed sloth, but I don't remember what it was.

The last thing I wanted to think about right now was mating habits.

Waiting for the last bell in homeroom, I reflected on how confident and optimistic I'd been this morning — just a few short hours ago. I was going to Act As If I'd already made Adam fall in love with me. I was going to be secure in my love-ability. This was the day I was to have taken Life by the scruff of the neck and shaken it till I got what I wanted. What a joke. Life was probably laughing up its sleeve at me right now.

The last bell rang. I hauled myself out of my seat. I trudged out the door of my homeroom, my shoulders slumping with the weight of my despair. It had to be despair; my books weren't all that heavy.

Adam was at his locker. He was opening his locker and taking books out and putting books in. He was hardly ever at his locker at three o'clock, but here he was today.

And that wasn't all. Leaning against my locker, her back to me but her limp, muddy-blond hair instantly recognizable, was Mary Louise Dryden.

If I didn't need my jacket; if I didn't need my biology book, which I'd forgotten to get after lunch; if I didn't have a reading assignment in English, I would have turned around and run down the south stairs without going near my locker.

But it was 38 degrees out; we had a test in biology on Monday, which I'd known about for a week, but had been too busy to bother about. . . .

I took a deep breath and strode to my locker. Adam was just slamming his shut. Mary Louise was still propped against mine.

"Hi," said Adam. His voice was kind of soft and tentative. I figured he was so dazzled by Mary Louise (???) that he could hardly talk.

"Hi," I said.

Mary Louise turned around. Her watery blue eyes looked right through me as if I weren't there.

"Excuse me," I said coolly, "but that's my locker. Could you move a little?"

Mary Louise shuffled her combat boots sideways, which brought her a foot closer to Adam. Not exactly what I had in mind, but really, what difference did it make? She was already closer to Adam than I'd ever be.

I struggled with my lock because I couldn't see the numbers too well and my fingers were trembling along with most of the rest of my body. Suddenly a familiar voice behind me boomed, "Hey, Adam!"

"Hey, Terry!"

I whirled around and found myself nose to nose with Terence Malley.

"You scared me," I blurted out.

Then it hit me. *"Hey, Adam." "Hey, Terry."*

Terence actually knew Adam Holmquist. *Had* known him. Had known him all along, maybe. Could have introduced me. Could have — oh, I couldn't stand it! More *ifs*. And now it was too late.

"I was worried about you, Maddy," Terence said. "You seemed so down today. You didn't say a word to me all day. I mean, not even when I told you about the sloths, and that's a sure-fire grabber."

I scowled at him. For some reason, Adam and Mary Louise were still standing there, hearing every word of this. I wished Terence would disappear. I wished *I* would disappear. I could not get that stupid locker open. I rattled the lock, grabbed the handle, and shook it furiously.

Terence did not disappear. Terence continued talking. "So, what's wrong? Want to talk about it with old Uncle Terry?"

"Terence," I said, in a choked little voice, "what's wrong is that I can't get this stinking locker open." I yanked at the handle again.

"Sometimes," said Mary Louise disinterestedly,

"you have to kick it." She took two short steps to my locker, drew her foot back, and bashed the bottom of my locker with the toe of her combat boot.

Terence pulled the handle and the door opened. Adam looked positively enthralled by Mary Louise's footwork.

"Ready, Adam?" Mary Louise said. Her voice was utterly toneless. She could have been asking for a pound of liver.

"Oh, yeah, sure," Adam said absently. "See you," he said to me. I was surprised he knew I was there. "Take care, Ter."

"Take care," Ter said.

They walked off together. Just like Beauty and the Beast, Romeo and Zelda, Robert Redford and Phyllis Diller.

I threw the books I was holding into the locker, right on top of the books I should have been taking home. I pulled out my jacket.

"Hey, hey, we have a test in biology," Terence reminded me. "Aren't you going to take the book home? And the Spanish homework. We have to —"

I sniffled. I couldn't help it. I would *not cry*, I told myself, but I just couldn't help that little sniffle. My heart was — this time — definitely and permanently broken, and I was entitled to a sniffle at the very least.

Little though it was, Terence heard it. "Hey, come on, what is it? It can't be that bad. Here, let me get your books, you'll need them." He leaned into my locker to reach for my biology book and my notebook.

"I don't want them!" I grabbed the locker door and started to slam it. I nearly closed it on his neck, but he leaped back just in time.

"Jeez, Maddy, what's with you today? You nearly took my head off. I'm just trying to help."

Something crumpled inside me. "I know," I whispered. "I'm sorry."

He looked at me strangely. At least, I think he did. My eyes were kind of blurred.

"I didn't know you knew Adam," he said casually.

"I don't."

"Nice guy."

"I didn't know *you* knew him," I said, trying to sound normal.

"He just moved here in August," Terence said. "He lives down the block from me."

Down the block from him?

Terence sort of pushed me toward the south stairs. I stumbled along blindly.

"Uh, listen, Maddy, you're not on anything, are you?"

"No!" I cried indignantly. "Of course not!"

"Okay, okay. But I'd better make sure you get home all right. You are really in rotten shape today."

We walked outside. Terence bundled me into my jacket. I could have managed to put on my own jacket.

"I don't need any help getting home," I said. "There's nothing wrong with me."

"All right. There's nothing wrong with you. But you don't mind if I just walk with you, do you? Did you know that in Oklahoma it's against the law to get a fish drunk?"

The music began and Estrellita whirled into the center of the ballroom, clicking her castanets and flashing her black eyes at the guests. She danced with wild abandon, her red skirts swirling to reveal glimpses of her long, bare legs.

Her black hair tumbled over her olive shoulders as she flung her head forward. The tempo of the music increased and the gypsy girl's dance grew wilder.

Beside her, Doña Veronica heard Ernesto draw his breath in sharply. She could not help turning to glance at him. He was not even aware she was looking. His eyes were riveted on Estrellita. His mouth was slightly open, his hands clenched at his sides.

He was besotted, the fool! Besotted still — or again — with the shameless gypsy hussy who had inflamed him so many years ago.

Jealously flared in Doña Veronica, mad, unreasoning jealously. I hate him, she told herself, I hate him. How can I possibly be jealous of the infatuations of his youth?

The music built to a dramatic crescendo and Estrellita whirled dizzyingly around the floor. At the final throb of the drum, she flung herself at Ernesto's feet, tearing the rose from her hair. She dropped her head back to the floor and stretched her arm upward, offering the flower to Ernesto.

As the guests burst into applause, Doña Veronica saw a little smile play upon Ernesto's lips. He

*reached down and plucked the rose from Estrellita's
tapering fingers. . . .*

Sure, Estrellita the flashy gypsy girl might give
Doña Veronica a run for her money — and for
Ernesto — but *Mary Louise Dryden?* If Mary Louise
Dryden ever took a man away from Doña Veronica
I'd bet anything that Doña Veronica would sell her
wardrobe, toss her black lace fans into the Rio
Grande, and tuck herself back into that convent.

Besotted. What a good word! That's just what
Adam was — besotted. With . . . *Mary Louise Dryden?*

It was going to drive me crazy. I was utterly
miserable. I moved through the weekend like a
sleepwalker groping in the fog. I didn't care that I
was going to fail Monday's biology test and get a
zero for not doing the Spanish homework. I didn't
care that we were supposed to read twenty pages of
something or other for English. All I cared about
was why in the world Adam Holmquist was —
heaven help me — besotted with Mary Louise
Dryden.

She was bright. Maybe he liked bright girls.

But there were plenty of intelligent, great-looking
girls at Longley. Erin Coughlin for one. Well, she
was going with Tom Noonan, but there were
others.

Maybe he had a combat boot fetish.

That's ridiculous.

Isn't it?

Maybe Karen was right. Maybe Mary Louise had

some certain, indefinable "Genie says kwoy" that sparked a sort of automatic chemical/biological reaction in Adam. Say it was something else nobody could see, or nobody else was sensitive to. Like, some people are allergic to tomatoes. Something in their body is susceptible to something in tomatoes, and they get a rash. Maybe something in Adam is susceptible to something in Mary Louise, and —

It was too disgusting to think about.

Terence had really been very nice Friday afternoon. He'd chattered at me all the way home, telling me as many interesting facts about sloths, etc., as he could think of, and reminding me that I had actually asked him to come up with more of these tidbits.

I couldn't tell him, but that was B.M.L. (Before Mary Louise.) Now I didn't need to hear about armadillos, sloths, the fattest U.S. President, and how you can tell male and female turtles apart.

Besides which, it occurred to me Friday night that if Adam had known Terence since August, he'd already heard those dumb things I'd told him about the gay seagulls and the armadillos.

He was just being polite the day before, when he said how interesting it all was. He already *knew* that armadillos get leprosy. Terence probably told him that one the first time they met.

"Hi, there. New in the neighborhood? My name's Terence Malley. Did you know that apart from man, the armadillo is the only animal that can get leprosy?"

And then up comes Maddy, two months later, with exactly the same line. And what are the odds against entering a new school and having two separate people tell you exactly the same thing about armadillos? Maybe that certain, indefinable quality Mary Louise had was that she didn't talk about armadillos. Or much of anything else, for that matter. Maybe Adam liked the strong silent type.

I was stretched out on my bed Sunday afternoon trying to free my mind from its obsession with Adam and Mary Louise by reading *Sweet, Suffering Love*. It wasn't working too well. I kept having to go back and reread whole paragraphs. Even paragraphs that were chock-full of fire images.

The phone rang.

"I have shirshayed la femme!"

"You have what?"

"Shirshayed la femme," Karen repeated impatiently. "That's French."

"Not as we know it. What do you mean, anyway? What woman have you shirshayed?"

"The one whose name you won't let me say."

"Mary Louise Dryden? I don't understand what you're talking about. She wasn't lost. Unfortunately."

"Just listen, will you? Listen to what happened. You know I'm having trouble with geometry, right? So my mother called the head of the math department at school and asked for a student tutor for me. So she got a list of four names and she told me to pick one, but I didn't really want a tutor in the first place, so I didn't even bother to look at the list until today when she got really threatening about it —"

"So?"

"Mary Louise was one of the names on the list!"

"Well, what of it? We knew she was smart."

"Don't you get it? It explains everything."

"Karen, I don't know what you're talking about."

"She's Adam's tutor! That's why he was with her. They were probably making an appointment for her to tutor him! He must be having trouble with trig or calculus or whatever it is seniors have to take."

Could it be? My fingers tightened around the receiver. My mouth went dry. It would explain everything. They were probably going right over to Adam's after school and that's why she was with him then. And in the morning they were arranging the appointment, just as Karen said.

"Maddy? You still there?"

"Oh, yeah. Sure. I was just thinking."

"Well, that's got to be it, right? I mean, what else could it be? That's the only explanation. And what a lucky coincidence! I mean, if I wasn't failing geometry, we'd never have known."

"Every cloud has a silver lining," I said. "It's an ill wind that blows nobody any good."

"Right!" Karen sounded positively cheerful about failing geometry. That's a true friend, I thought.

"Karen, thanks a million. I really appreciate it."

"Anytime," she said. "Bon soyer."

"Bon soyer. See you tomorrow."

I hung up the phone and leaned back against the wall behind my bed. Did it explain everything? Not quite. What about Adam's dopey, *besotted* look when Mary Louise was at his locker? What about his soft, mushy voice, barely able to mumble a "Hi" to me when she was standing a foot away from him?

I sighed and reached for my copy of *Seven Days*

to a Brand-new You. Terence might be able to tell me if Mary Louise was tutoring Adam. I could ask him sort of casually tomorrow. But even if the tutoring explained a lot, it didn't explain everything. Maybe there are things in life that never get explained. It seemed as if I might still have a ray of hope, a ghost of a chance, a one in a million shot to get Adam besotted over me — and I only had two more days to go to complete the seven days of my program.

Besides, I told myself, turning to "Day Six," even if I never do drive Adam out of his gourd, there are plenty of good reasons to go on creating the Brand-new Me. Even without Adam, a popular, outgoing, confident new me would certainly get more out of life than the old me. I'd gone this far; what did I have to lose by finishing what I'd started?

Doña Veronica would never give up so easily. I tossed my head back defiantly like Doña Veronica and started to read "Day Six."

Day Six

Rome wasn't built in a day, you know. Perhaps everything did not go as you planned yesterday. What went wrong? Study your mistakes. Learn from your failures — and try again! Remember, you can GET WHAT YOU WANT. You deserve it!

O R, to put it another way, if at first you don't succeed, try, try again. I was getting a little p.o.'d with Dr. Dudley. As far as I could tell, I hadn't made any mistakes Friday. I never got the chance to make any. What went wrong was that out of nowhere, Mary Louise Dryden appeared and I had no control over that.

Aha! But how did I act after she turned up? Did I project confidence, love-ability, charm, etc.? Did I Act As If Adam were already mine?

No. I gave up on the spot. I threw in the towel.

I forgot everything I was supposed to be doing on Day Five and instead of Acting As If I were a dynamic, successful, capable, irresistible person, I had acted as if I were a spoiled child sulking over a lost Monopoly game. I had — in my mind — gone to my room and slammed the door. Not just on Adam, but on everybody.

That was a mistake. I shouldn't have let one little setback wipe out all the good work I'd done up until now. As a matter of fact — and wouldn't Dr. Dudley be proud of me for thinking of this — that setback ought to prod me into a new determination. I would redouble my efforts. Maybe Mary Louise was Adam's tutor or maybe she *did* have Adam wrapped around her nail-bitten little finger. It didn't matter either way. I'd radiate confidence, charm, love-ability, cheerfulness, all that stuff until I was blue in the face. And not just to Adam. To everybody.

Sure, Adam was the big prize, the brass ring, the whipped cream on the sundae. Sure, I wanted him more than anything or anyone else. But there was a whole school out there, and beyond that, a whole world. If, by some unjust twist of fate, I didn't get Adam to fall madly in love with me, it sure would help to know that a whole slew of other boys had.

That was what I told myself, and almost believed, as I walked to school. Of course, between the sentences of this pep talk I was giving myself, stray thoughts crept in like mice and began to nibble away at my confidence, and determination.

Would Adam be at his locker? Would Mary Louise be there with him? Was Mary Louise really just a hired employee, guiding Adam through the intricacies of Math 12? Even if she were, did she have her eye on him for herself? Was she, at this very moment, waging her own campaign to drive Adam out of his gourd? If not, why not? Was the girl *blind* as well as everything else?

I tried very hard to dismiss these thoughts from my mind as I went upstairs to my locker. I told myself they were counterproductive. What I am going to think about now, I reminded myself, is being the Brand-new Me and dazzling the school populace in general.

The halls were pretty crowded, so when I got to the second floor I couldn't see right away whether Adam was there. But I didn't crane my neck, push through the throngs, exhibit any anxiety whatsoever. I strolled casually, confidently down the hall, smiling at everyone who looked even vaguely familiar, and calling out a cheerful "Hello" to everyone who looked more than vaguely familiar. When I knew their names, I added them to the "Hello." "Hi, Doris, Jack, Tracey . . ." or whoever. I must say I was kind of surprised at how surprised most of them were. People certainly weren't used to the New Me yet. Well, how could they be? I hadn't given them the chance.

But after the initial shock that it was indeed me, Madeline Kemper the (formerly) quiet, greeting them so heartily, most people responded with more warmth than I'd expected. I mean, some of them even said more than just "Hi." Some even added, "How you doing?" or "See you in English."

It really felt good walking among all those people

with my head up to see all the smiles I was getting in return for mine. Maybe Dr. Dudley wasn't such a dud after all.

And finally, I was at my locker.

And Adam wasn't.

I know my smile disappeared. I could almost feel my shoulders slump. Good-bye, confidence. So long, charm.

NO! No no no no *no*. Determination. I have just begun to fight. Don't give up the ship. I'll fight it out on this line if it takes all winter. Faint heart ne'er won fair man. Don't fire until you see the whites of their eyes. (That can't be right.)

"Hi there. Feel better?"

Terence Malley was leaning against my locker. Had he seen my smile turn to sorrow? Had he seen my shoulders slump? Had he seen me bidding a tearful farewell to confidence and charm? And did he think it was because I was unhappy to see him? That would be terrible. Of course, I *was* unhappy to see him, but only because he wasn't Adam.

And that wasn't his fault.

I pasted the smile back on my lips.

"Hi, Terence! Sure, I feel fine." I was amazed at how well I was faking cheerfulness.

I twirled my combination lock and pulled on the handle of the locker. Nothing happened.

Terence stepped back a bit and raised his foot.

"May I?" he asked formally.

"Be my guest."

He smashed his foot into the base of the locker. He pulled at the handle. Nothing happened.

"I think you have to get it at a certain spot," I said, "just above the little slits."

"Well, uh, listen, Maddy, this is kind of embarrassing, but —"

"Oh, don't be silly, Terence. Just because you can't open my locker — I mean, nobody can open this locker."

"It's not that." He winced. "I forgot I was wearing sneakers. I think I broke my toes."

I couldn't help it. I began to laugh and I just couldn't stop. Poor Terence was hobbling around in a little circle going "Ooh, ouch, oh, God," and I was clutching my arms to my stomach and having hysterics.

"You won't believe this," I gasped finally, "but I know exactly how you feel."

"Yeah, I can tell."

"I'm sorry" was all I managed before I started laughing again.

"You think it's funny that I broke my toes. Sure. I can understand that. Why not?" He was still grimacing in pain and trying to touch his foot to the ground. "What could be funnier than five broken toes? Ten broken toes maybe. The whole leg? Stick around; you're gonna love this. For an encore I rupture my spleen. Oh, God, I'll never play soccer again."

I was finally under control. "I didn't know you played soccer."

"I used to," he said tersely. He leaned against the lockers and held his ankle. "Now I just hop."

"I'm sorry, It's only that everybody breaks their toes on this locker."

"Really? How interesting."

"Now, Terence, don't be mad. Why I was laughing was that the exact same thing happened to me a couple of days ago. I mean, exactly. When I said I knew how you felt, I really *did*. And my toes weren't broken, so yours probably aren't either."

"Were you wearing sneakers?"

"Well, no, I —"

"Then don't you think you ought to leave the diagnosis up to a doctor?"

"You want to go down to the nurse's office? I'll help you."

He let go of his ankle and put his foot to the floor.

"No. I think it's feeling a little better. Boy, try and do a person a favor."

"I appreciate it, Terence. I really do. And I'm sorry I —"

"Hi . . . Madeline."

There was no time to gasp. While I'd been talking to Terence, this gorgeous vision had materialized right next to me and I hadn't even noticed. Hi, *Madeline?* How did he know my name? Where was Mary Louise? Why is he talking like this, in that soft, hesitant voice when she isn't here?

I wanted to gulp, but there was no time for that either.

Confidence. Charm. Irresistibleness. (Irresistibleness? Is that a word? WHO CARES? Just *be* it.) I'm going to faint. I'm going to choke up. I always choke up in a crisis. No I don't. That was the Old Madeline. Get to it already!

"Hi there!" It wasn't much, but it beat fainting.

And it gave me a few seconds to think up something else.

"Having trouble with that locker again?"

He had his open already. What a man!

And with incredibly quick thinking, especially for me, I said, "It's really acting up this morning. I think it's got arthritis or something."

"Did you kick it?"

"One of us did," Terence said sourly.

"Let me try it," Adam offered.

"You better be wearing lead shoes," Terence snarled.

"Oh, yeah, be careful," I said. "Poor Terence nearly broke his toes on that stupid door."

"What nearly?" Terence demanded. "It has not yet been determined whether or not my toes are broken."

Adam turned to Terence. "You really hurt? You want me to help you down to the nurse's office or something?"

The first bell rang.

"No, thanks. Poor Terence will make it to his homeroom on his own one foot. Just see if you can get that locker open for her, will you? She has a biology test and if she starts studying during the Pledge of Allegiance and skips lunch, she might get a thirty-six on it."

What in the world was the matter with Terence? He sounded so bitter — and at the same time, why did he care whether I got a thirty-six or a ninety-six on my biology test?

"I forgot all about that stupid test," I said softly. I didn't care all that much about it right now — not with Adam standing this close to me, ready to sacrifice his toes for my locker, and Terence scowling on the other side of me for some mysterious reason. But I thought I ought to sound as if I cared a *little*.

Besides, it was something to say.

"I know," Terence said. He wasn't scowling now and his voice wasn't harsh anymore. "You had other things on your mind. See you later."

He hobbled off down the hall.

Leaving me alone (except for the other thirty or so people in the corridor) with Adam.

"Okay, run through the full combination again," Adam said, "and then we'll give it a kick."

"I hope 'we' means you," I said. "The last time I kicked it was the last time I'll *ever* kick it." I continued to be amazed at my lightning wit. It might not sound that great to anyone else, but believe me, for me it was terrific.

Another amazing thing was that although my heart was definitely pounding loud enough to be heard over the roar of a speeding locomotive (and beating faster than the speeding locomotive, I might add), my hands did not shake as I turned the lock. Well, not very much, anyway. I mean, here he is, and here I am, and here Mary Louise isn't, and he's talking to me and struggling with my locker and he knows my name and the first bell has already rung and he has two minutes left to get to his own homeroom but he's still here, and I might faint after all.

"Seventeen right," I said weakly. "There you go."

He kicked my locker.

He pulled the handle.

Nothing happened.

He rattled the handle. Nothing.

"This is worse than mine," he said.

"This is worse than anybody's. I think we're going to need a blowtorch to get this opened. We better forget about it for now. You're going to be late."

"Oh, that's okay. But what about your test?"

I smiled ruefully. "To tell you the truth, even if I did study from now till seventh period, I probably wouldn't pass it."

To tell you the truth, I DON'T CARE!

I will later, I will next week when the marks come back, I will when my parents see my report card, but right now?

"Well. Sorry I couldn't help. See you later then. Take care."

Take care. What beautiful words. What a beautiful phrase. Everybody says it, but have you ever stopped to analyze it? The implications of it?

Take care. Take care of yourself. "Take good care of yourself, you belong to me."

Oh, yes. Oh, yes I do, Adam. And I will. I will take care. I will take care of myself. And, if necessary, though it doesn't seem all that likely now, I'll take care of Mary Louise Dryden, too.

Despite the fact that I positively floated from class to class all morning — which is not easy in a crowded hallway — despite the fact that I was *besotted* with all Adam's attention, I still managed to remember to project my dynamic new personality.

And for some reason it got easier and easier to act

friendly and cheerful to everyone. Of course, the more you do something, the easier it's supposed to get, but it wasn't just that.

The love I felt for Adam and the optimism generated by this morning's little tête-à-tête at my locker spread throughout my entire being and somehow radiated outward into a general feeling of love for all personkind.

And it must have showed, because personkind returned my good cheer and then some. I was a walking, talking greeting card, spreading my little rays of sunshine wherever I went, and collecting little rays of sunshine back from people who had never said two words to me before. (Possibly because I'd never said two words to *them* before.)

People are wonderful, I thought that morning. People are wonderful, life is wonderful, Dr. Dudley is wonderful, everything's coming up roses, life is just a bowl of cherries. . . .

Of course, there was the minor problem of not having done my Spanish homework.

"I couldn't get my locker open," I told Señora Schacter. Well, it was the truth. I didn't say I'd *done* my homework and it was in there.

"Terence tried, and he couldn't get it open either; right, Terence?"

"*That's* true," Terence said wryly.

"You'd better get a custodian to open it for you," Señora Schacter said, "and bring in the assignment tomorrow."

"Yes, I will. I definitely will, *Gracias,* Señora Schacter."

"That was quick thinking," Terence said, with

grudging admiration, as Señora Schacter turned to the blackboard. "Devious, but quick thinking."

"Yes. It seems to be my specialty today. I'm dazzling myself with my own footwork. Speaking of footwork, how are your toes?"

"Still attached to my feet."

"And the rest of you?" I asked pointedly. "You were acting a little weird this morning."

"Well, now we're even. You were acting weird Friday."

"What do you mean, weird?" I demanded. "I thought I was acting very nice."

"You are. That's what's weird."

I shrugged impatiently and gave up.

"My friends!" I cried, as I sat down with my lunch tray. "And you *are* my friends," I went on, in the manner of a campaigning congressperson. "While we break bread together —"

"You can't break this bread," Sandy said. "The best you can do is hit it with a blunt instrument."

"While we enjoy this delicious meal —"

"Are we eating the same thing?" Barbara cut in.

"While we lunch here in sisterhood and solidarity —"

"What is with you today?" demanded Sandy.

"I'm happy, for heaven's sake! I'm a Little Mary Sunshine, spreading goodwill wherever I go."

Sandy studied my face critically. "I think," she said, "I liked you better depressed."

I patted her hand affectionately. "Silly Sandy."

"I *definitely* liked you better depressed."

"I know!" Karen cried. "I know what it is. It's *him*. Isn't it him, Maddy?"

"Indeed it is. Cherchez la — what's French for 'man'?"

" 'Home,' " said Karen.

"Yes. Cherchez la home. That's it exactly."

"Something happened!" Barbara said excitedly. "What? Did he talk to you?"

"Did *you* talk to *him?*" Sandy asked.

"We both talked to each other," I said calmly. "And he kicked my locker for me. And he was late to homeroom because of me."

"Greater love hath no man," Sandy said. But she seemed impressed. "Okay: From the beginning."

It was a marvelous lunch.

Seventh period came, inevitably, and I did not float to biology. The test I was about to fail cast a little cloud over my otherwise sunny mood. Even though I was besotted, I was not besotted enough to loss *all* contact with reality.

I took my seat and started to get nervous. Was it possible that I could pass this test without having studied?

Can I walk on water?

If — I should say, when — I failed the test, and it was averaged in with the rest of my grades, would it affect my mark for the quarter very much?

Considering I had barely a "C" average so far, it sure wouldn't help.

Terence walked into the room. He didn't seem to be favoring his foot any. He headed straight for my desk. He leaned down, and in good old normal

Terence tones said, "Did you know that unborn babies can get the hiccups?"

"No. Is it going to be on the test?"

I told Mrs. Frank about how I couldn't get my locker open. She told me I had had a week to study for the test. Had I been unable to get my locker open for a week?

I glanced at Terence. He shrugged.

It was a fill-in-the-blanks test. With multiple choice I might have had a one out of four chance on each question. Having to fill in the blanks when my mind was a blank left me without a prayer.

Oh, well, I thought. Cest la vee, as Karen would say. I'll study twice as hard for the next test.

I hadn't studied at *all* for this one and two times zero is zero, but who had time to think logically now? Eighth period would be next and then school would be over and I'd see Adam and . . . and . . . ? Fill in the blank.

I made small talk in the eight minutes we had to stay in homeroom before school officially ended, never once letting on to the people I chatted with that I couldn't wait to get out of there and make small talk (or large, important talk) with Adam. Who would be waiting for me at our lockers. (I hoped. I prayed.)

Yes, indeedy, I still loved all personkind. But personkind in general did not make my knees turn to butter, my temperature rise, my heart soar, as did one person in particular.

The last bell rang — at last. I'm afraid I vaulted out of my seat as if I'd been launched by a slingshot.

I waved a cheery good-bye to my homeroom-mates with one arm and elbowed my way past them to the door with the other.

I sprinted down the hall to my locker. Adam wasn't there. Of course, I was awfully early. I had probably broken the record for the 50-locker dash from a seated start.

Since there was no point in attempting to open my locker, I lounged against it and tried to look casual. I applied some "Moist Mulberries" and flashed my toothpaste commercial smile.

And then Adam was coming toward me.

With Mary Louise at his side.

And I was now a "Before" picture in an acid stomach ad.

But only briefly. Remember this morning. You didn't imagine this morning. It really happened. Remember, you said you could take care of Mary Louise if you had to. Act As If. Ignore Mary Louise and flash on Adam.

"Hi . . . Madeline. Got that locker open yet?"

Someday this romance would progress beyond discussions of lockers, armadillos, and seagulls. Someday, I sighed, but not right this minute. Not with old Mary Louise standing there and almost glaring at me with her watery eyes.

I gave Adam a dazzling smile. I wanted to bare my teeth at Mary Louise, but not while Adam could see my fangs. She was standing close enough to him so that their sleeves touched.

It was then I discovered that it is not possible to love all personkind.

"No, I have to get a custodian to do it. And I

forgot all about it." Well, I couldn't help it. I had other things on my mind. There goes the Spanish homework. And the English reading. We won't even think about geometry. Especially not about triangles.

"You want me to kick it?" Mary Louise asked coldly.

"No thank you," I said, keeping the snarl out of my voice only with a great effort of will. "Adam already tried, and if *he* couldn't get it to open . . ."

I gazed up at Adam worshipfully and had to lower my eyes in confusion when I realized he was gazing down at *me*.

"I got it open yesterday," Mary Louise growled.

"Yeah, she did," Adam said softly. "Let her try it."

"If you insist." I clenched my teeth and worked the combination. I stood back and gestured toward the locker. "Feel free."

She raised her combat boot.

If she succeeded in getting that locker open I'd kill her with my bare hands.

She kicked the locker. I pulled the handle. It didn't open.

I tried to look disappointed.

I failed.

"Well, cest la vee," I chirped. "You tried, anyway."

Adam opened his locker and took out some books and his jacket. "You'd better get somebody to take care of that," he said. "Before your next test, anyway. Oh, hey — how did the test go?"

He cared! He *cared!* Whatever Mary Louise was doing it was no match for the Brand-new Me. He was talking to me, not her. He was practically ignoring her. Dumb old Mary Louise.

"Don't ask," I moaned. "If 'Four' is passing, I'm in good shape."

"You got a 'Four'?"

"Well, I got at least a 'Four.' I might have gotten as high as a 'Twelve.' "

Mary Louise looked at me with contempt.

"That's rough," Adam said sympathetically.

"Yeah, it sure is." I tried to look crushed. It wasn't easy because even with Mary Louise's malign presence blighting the otherwise gorgeous view, I felt terrific. But Adam seemed to expect me to feel devastated by my poor showing in biology, and I certainly wanted to live up to Adam's expectations.

"Come on, Adam, let's go," Mary Louise said impatiently. Dumb, damn Mary Louise.

But now he'd tell her! Now he'd say, "Look, you go. I want to stay here and talk some more with this incredible person who has just driven me right out of my gourd."

"Okay. Guess we'd better." Adam tucked his books under his arm.

Okay? *Okay?* That's not what you're supposed to say. That's not in the script I just wrote for you. You're supposed to say, "I want to stay here and ——"

"See you tomorrow, Madeline," Adam said. Did I detect a note of yearning in his voice? A look of reluctance in his eyes? As if he didn't really want to go with dumb damn Mary Louise, but for some unspeakable reason, had to?

Or was I just imagining it?

Courage, Madeline. Determination, positive thinking, Acting As If.

"I'll be here," I said airily. "Same time, same place. You'll recognize me because I'll be the one with the blowtorch."

He smiled. And then he said, "I'd recognize you without the blowtorch." And looked away quickly, almost as if he were embarrassed.

Mary Louise practically dragged him off down the hall. And I practically slithered to the floor in a little heap.

"Take your Estrellita and welcome to her!" cried Doña Veronica. "I am your wife in name only, after all. I expect nothing from you. Nothing! And my expectations have been thoroughly fulfilled."

Ernesto smiled sardonically. "Nothing, mi querida? Have you forgotten the night the revolutionaries set fire to the governor's palacio and we —"

"I have forgotten nothing! Not one moment of my sordid existence with you, you — you — "

"Can it be that at last you are jealous, mi esposa? Oh, I like that. I like it very much. It means that you care for me."

"I care nothing for you! Jealous? Hahaha!" Her laugh was wild and uncontrolled. "Go! Go off with your gypsy girl and leave me in peace at last."

Ernesto seized Doña Veronica around the waist and crushed her to his chest. He could feel her heart pounding through the bodice of her ivory brocade gown.

(That woman has not worn the same dress twice in this entire book.)

"I will never leave you. Never. You are mi vida, my life. You are all I have ever wanted. I will be with you till my last dying breath passes my lips."

He brought his mouth down passionately on hers. Doña Veronica gasped and nearly swooned in the heat of his embrace.

"Say that you do not love me," he ordered. "Say it, and I will believe it. But you must say it."

With a final cry of defeat, Doña Veronica threw her arms around Ernesto's neck. "I cannot," she whispered brokenly. "I cannot speak a lie."

(Chalk up another one for the convent.)

"At last, at last, my love!"
"Yes, Ernesto. At last and forever. . . ."

I assume they lived happily ever after, except for occasional hurling of crockery, brandishing of daggers, and a certain amount of ritual cloak-ripping.

I sighed and closed the book. What a great life Doña Veronica had had. What adventure, what romance, what clothes!

What stamina!

I tried very hard, but I couldn't really imagine Adam acting at all like Ernesto. I thought it was

93

pretty obvious by now that Adam was shy. No matter how hard I tried, I couldn't imagine (while I was awake, anyhow) Adam riding down the halls of Longley on a palomino, sweeping me up into the saddle, and riding off into the sunset. (Assuming the horse could make it down the south stairs.)

No, but my life was getting a lot more interesting than it had been when I'd started reading *Sweet, Suffering Love.*

Whatever Mary Louise had that Adam needed, it was not in the same category as what Estrellita the gypsy dancer had. Now, maybe Mary Louise wanted Adam, but the way he'd acted this afternoon, I was sure he had at least a passing interest in whatever it was *I* had.

Karen's explanation was really beginning to be the most believable. Adam had to leave with Mary Louise because she was tutoring him, which made her the teacher and him the obeyer. And Mary Louise, not being blind and possessing some normal human emotions, had succumbed to Adam's Greek-godliness.

Therefore, the way I saw it, Mary Louise craved Adam as a sex object, and Adam looked on Mary Louise as a way to pass Math 12.

I'd vowed this morning that I could take care of Mary Louise if necessary, but I really couldn't think how. Adam would have to handle that part of it. I mean, it was his problem if he didn't want her, but wanted me. (Oh, what a glorious thought.) After all, what could I do? The girl wears combat boots.

Doña Veronica had slapped Estrellita's face, but

Doña Veronica was nobility and Estrellita a peasant. You could do those things then. If Estrellita had hit back, she would have been clapped into jail for assaulting a nobleperson, which was a revolutionary act.

Too bad. I would enjoy very much socking Mary Louise. I would enjoy even more having her clapped into jail and out of my way. But force was out of the question. Either Adam would have to do something, or I'd have to outwit her, outcharm her, outdazzle her. But after all, how hard could that be?

I mean, Mary Louise Dryden, for heaven's sake!

Day Seven

A brand-new YOU, a brand-new life! These past seven days have set the pattern for a future filled with all the good things that life has to offer. The new YOU can have anything you want. Your last assignment for your Seven-Day Plan is to look at yourself in the mirror and say, "Hello, New Me. I am terrific. I am successful. I can have it ALL!" Even though your Seven-Day Plan is on its final day, a few minutes spent every morning from now on, repeating these magic phrases to yourself, will help you to maintain the NEW YOU in peak condition.

Today is the first day of the BEST of your life!

H ELLO, NEW ME."

The New Me didn't answer.

I smiled dazzlingly at the mirror.

"I am terrific! I am successful! I can have it all!"

"Maddy?" my mother called. "What are you doing on the phone at this hour?"

"I'm not on the phone. I'm talking to myself."

She opened the door and peered into my room. "Are you all right? Is anything wrong?"

"Not a thing. I'm fine. I'm terrific!"

She looked at me strangely. "That's good. You certainly have had the oddest mood changes these past few days."

"Well, from now on everything is going to be terrific."

"That may be the oddest one of all," she muttered. "But it's a fine attitude," she added hastily.

I left for school a little early because I remembered that I had not done a thing about getting a custodian to help me open my locker. And Señora Schacter expected the Spanish homework that was due yesterday. And I still hadn't done my reading for English. If I could get the Spanish finished in homeroom, maybe I could read straight through lunch, and get the English assignment done.

I stopped in at the main office and told one of the secretaries I couldn't get my locker open.

"What's the number?"

"Two-forty-eight."

"All right. I'll get a custodian to open it." She turned back to her paper sorting.

"Uh, could you do it fast, please? I really need my stuff."

"As soon as possible." She continued to sort papers.

"I haven't been able to get into it for two days, and my homework and all —"

"As soon as possible," she repeated sternly. She began evening up the stacks of paper.

"Yeah. Thanks a lot."

When Dr. Dudley said the New Me could get anything I wanted out of life, he obviously did not realize I might want something from a school secretary.

I went upstairs to my locker to await the arrival of the custodian and Adam — not necessarily in that order.

I passed the time waving to people and repeating Dr. Dudley's magic phrases — along with a few others — in my head.

"I am wonderful," I told myself. "I am lovable. I can have anything I want, including Adam. Adam likes me. I know he does. He does not like Mary Louise Dryden because Mary Louise Dryden is a toad. He only went with her yesterday because she had to give him his math lesson. He really wanted to stay and talk to me. But business before pleasure. Then again, all work and no play makes Adam a dull boy. Come on out and play, Adam! So what if you fail Math 12? I'm going to fail biology, and misery loves company.

"I am terrific. I am successful. I can have anything I want."

"Where's your blowtorch?" Adam's soft voice roused me from my thoughts. I hadn't even seen him coming. Mary Louise was not with him.

But Terence was.

"My blowtorch?" I repeated stupidly. Then I remembered my witticism of the day before. "Oh, that blowtorch. I decided to try a custodian before doing anything drastic. They're supposed to send one up here. You'll notice I'm not holding my breath."

Untrue. I was holding my breath throughout that entire speech.

Adam smiled. But didn't say anything.

We just sort of stood there for a while, smiling shyly at each other. I couldn't think of anything else to say, and besides, wasn't it Adam's turn? I mean, I'd just said four sentences all in a row and even the terrific New Me couldn't keep a conversation going without a *little* help.

Nothing elaborate. One simple sentence would do. "I love you madly" was a good start. Or, "You may not realize it, but you are driving me out of my gourd." Or even, "Wanna go to the movies?"

Finally Terence cleared his throat. "Did you know," he said, "that pound for pound, grasshoppers are three times as nutritious as steak?"

Why did Terence have to be there? Why was he butting into my private (if a little one-sided) conversation with Adam? Why did he keep offering these little gems at the most inopportune times? Why didn't he just *go away?*

"That's very interesting," Adam said. "About how many grasshoppers would you need to make a pound?"

Why was Adam talking to Terence instead of me? Why did he want to know how many grasshoppers you get in a pound?

I'm afraid I forgot every lesson I'd learned during my Seven-Day Plan. I forgot about projecting charm, love-ability and cheerfulness. I forgot about my love for all personkind.

I scowled at Terence.

It must have been one of my better scowls, because the corners of Terence's mouth turned down in what looked almost like . . . defeat?

"Better get going. See you. Thanks for the ride, Adam." He walked off down the hall. For a moment I felt terrible; I'd hurt his feelings, I was sure. Even though I hadn't said anything, he knew how I felt, knew that I wished he'd disappear and leave me alone with Adam.

But the moment passed. The implications of "Thanks for the ride" dawned on me.

Adam had a car! How perfect. How absolutely marvelous. Not only was he gorgeous, not only was he a wonderful person — I didn't know him very well, but he must be a wonderful person, otherwise how could I be so deeply in love with him? — but he had a *car* too!

That's shallow, Maddy, I told myself. That's really shallow. If he didn't have a car, would he be one bit less desirable?

Of course not. But having a car makes him one bit *more* desirable.

The first bell rang. We still hadn't exchanged any words beyond my first four sentences.

"I guess," I said, "the custodian isn't going to make it before my first class."

"Yeah. That's rough," Adam said. "What are you going to do?"

"I don't know. Try and stall my teachers for time, I guess."

If I'd thought about something other than Adam, I realized I could have borrowed Terence's Spanish book and done the homework. But it was very hard to think of practical matters with the boy of my dreams smiling shyly at me.

"Uh, well, look, I'll see you later, okay? I mean, you'll be here this afternoon?"

Whoops. I got a sinking feeling in my chest, which was undoubtedly my heart plunging down somewhere in the vicinity of my feet.

With great effort I made my voice light again. "Where else? I could be here forever, waiting for someone to open this thing."

"Good. I mean, not that you'll be here forever, I mean — I just sort of, uh — I mean if you want, I could drive you home."

"Oh." My voice was all soft and melty — very much like the rest of me. I could hardly believe that it was happening at last.

"That would be . . . great."

As I slid into my seat next to Terence in Spanish, I remembered for the first time since Adam offered to drive me home how guilty I felt about hurting Terence's feelings. I wanted to make it up to him somehow, to show him I really hadn't meant it. After all, it wasn't Terence's fault that he'd happened to be in the wrong place at the wrong time.

"So," I said briskly, "how many grasshoppers *does* it take to make a pound?"

He looked at me. A long, slow, meditative look.

"That's all right," he said gently. "I understand."

I fiddled with my pocketbook self-consciously. I wished I had some books to stack, or a notebook to flip through, or *something* to do with my hands to hide my discomfort.

"What do you mean, you understand?" I asked nervously. *"What* do you understand?"

"Everything," he said.

And I believed him.

He reached into his pocket and pulled out a crumpled litle piece of paper. He dropped it onto my desk.

"You might find this amusing," he said. "I found it in a fortune cookie."

I smoothed out the narrow strip and read: "Confucious say: Platonic love like being invited down to wine cellar for ginger ale."

Oh my.

I smoothed the paper over and over again with my fingers.

I cleared my throat. "It's — very amusing. Very clever. Was there, uh, some particular reason you wanted me to read this?"

He looked me square in the eye, but only for the briefest instant. Then he glanced away. "Think about it," he said.

I thought about it. I thought about it all through the rest of the day, when I wasn't thinking about riding home in Adam's car and having him tell me I had driven him right out of his gourd. And I thought about it even then, too, because the thoughts were really inseparable, intertwined.

All the time I'd been mooning around over Adam, Terence had been mooning around over me. It explained everything. He'd acted weird after he kicked my locker because he was annoyed seeing that I was more interested in Adam than in him.

Had my Seven-Day Plan been so effective that I not only besotted the boy I wanted, but the boy I hadn't wanted? If so, this was pretty potent stuff Dr. Dudley was peddling. The book ought to come with a warning label.

But Terence had always been nice to me. I mean, even when I was the Old Me, shy (with most people), withdrawn, sparrowish, Terence had been friendly. And when I'd been sarcastic about his pearls of arcane knowledge, he'd never minded. He'd enjoyed it. Had he liked me all along? If he had, why in the world had he waited until now to make a move?

Maybe because he hadn't felt pressed for time before this. Maybe because he saw I was falling for Adam and figured he'd have to do something quick. Or maybe it was even more basic that that. Maybe he'd liked me all along, but until Adam seemed to like me (maybe they even talked about me!) he didn't realize what an incredibly lovable, desirable, passion-provoking creature I now was.

Or maybe, I realized suddenly, the day that I'd asked him for more flaky facts, because Adam had asked me if I knew any more, Terence had taken that as a sign I was interested in him. After all, I'd taken it as a sign Adam was interested in *me*.

Life's little ironies. The quirky old God of Bad Timing had zapped me once again.

What was I going to do?

I didn't have the slightest idea. I had set a series of events in motion, purely out of a mad passion for a particular gorgeous person, and I certainly couldn't stem the tide now. I didn't want to. I was, maybe, finally, going to get in *real life* what I had only dreamed of before, and I got the most incredible shivers down my spine simply thinking about it.

You cannot deny shivers down your spine. You cannot turn your back on destiny. Especially not after you worked so hard to make destiny what you wanted it to be.

I didn't want to hurt Terence. But I couldn't help it if I didn't feel for him what I felt for Adam. And I just didn't.

What a tangle. I wanted Adam. Terence wanted me. Mary Louise wanted Adam. Adam wanted (I think, I hope, I'm almost positive) me. This was no longer a triangle; it was a rectangle. It was ridiculous.

I mean, whoever heard of a romantic *rectangle*, for heaven's sake?

By the time biology rolled around, I was feeling this tremendous compassion for Terence.

Poor Terence. Who better than I knew how it felt to suffer the pangs of unrequited love? I had practically been on the brink of self-destruction over Adam; I knew what Terence must be going through.

Who would have thought it? Me, shy, plain, (formerly) drab little Madeline Kemper had turned into a veritable heartbreaker. I hoped Terence wouldn't do anything drastic.

I wondered as I waited for Terence to make his entrance, whether he expected me to say anything about the fortune cookie message he'd shown me. He'd told me to think about it. Should I tell him I had, or should I just pretend the whole thing had never happened?

What if he asked me whether I'd thought about it? What then?

I would be very, very gentle. I would explain that at this particular moment a platonic relationship was all that was possible between us. (He already knew that anyhow.) I would tell him that I would always consider him a good friend. I would be sympathetic and understanding. And then maybe I could try and fix him up with Barbara. I thought they ought to get along pretty well. Perhaps she could help him get over me.

Terence came into the room. He walked toward my desk, head held high, a serious expression on his face.

Uh oh. I steeled myself for the moment of confrontation. No matter what sensible plans I had just made to deal with Terence's broken heart, I really wasn't prepared to be cool about it. After all, I'd never had any experience at being a heartbreaker before.

He leaned over my desk and looked deeply into my eyes. He put his hand gently on my shoulder.

I gulped. "Uh, listen, Terence, about that fortune cookie —"

His eyes shifted so that they were no longer meeting mine. He gazed off into the distance. The hand touching my shoulder gave it a little pat.

"Did you know," he said gravely, "that female aphids are born pregnant?"

For a moment I was too confused to speak. Then

I realized what he was doing. He was going to pretend nothing had ever happened between us. Well, nothing ever *had,* but he was going to pretend he'd never wanted anything to. He was going to be brave, strong, resigned to just being friends instead of lovers. He was going to mask his broken heart with a facade of casual quips, a cloak of feigned indifference. Oh, poor, brave Terence! I would help him keep up his false front. I would go right along with the pretense that his heart was not broken.

"If female aphids are born pregnant," I said, "how do male aphids have any fun?"

He frowned. "That never occurred to me," he said thoughtfully.

He walked back to his desk.

I twisted around in my seat, and saw him lean over to talk to Nancy Tedesco, a cute blonde with Little Orhpan Annie hair and big, round glasses.

Maybe I wouldn't have to fix him up with Barbara.

Nancy Tedesco was giggling. Terence was gesturing animatedly with his hands. He was obviously trying hard to get over me on his own.

I turned back in my seat. For a body with a broken heart, Terence was certainly putting on a good act. Of course, I was pleased that he was trying to work through his emotional crisis instead of moping around and suffering.

I didn't want Terence to suffer. At least, not *too* much. Doña Veronica may have driven three men to suicide because she didn't return their love, but I really didn't want to be responsible for anything so extreme.

There was, however, deep inside some dark little corner of my mind, the nasty, fleeting thought that I would rather Terence not recover from his heartbreak quite so quickly.

My homeroom teacher, Mr. Lutz, told me I could skip homeroom and go to my locker to wait for the custodian who had been promised to me a mere seven hours before.

On the off chance that the custodian had already been there and fixed it, I tried to open my locker. The custodian had not already been there and fixed it.

I sighed and leaned back. Only eight minutes to wait for Adam. Only eight minutes till he drives me home. Only eight minutes before he looks deeply into my eyes and confesses he's loved me all along.

Eight minutes. An eternity.

I looked at my watch. I waited, as four minutes crept by with agonizing slowness.

"Hi."

I looked up. Dazzled by his beauty, befuddled by his unexpectedly early appearance, I blurted out the first words that came into my head.

"You're too early."

He looked momentarily as confused as I felt.

"Uh — so are you," he said finally. "Or have you been waiting here all day?"

Did he think I'd stand by my locker all day waiting for him? Was he conceited? How could he be both shy and conceited? Had I been all that obvious about my crush on him when I wanted so to play it cool?

Of course, I *would* have stood by my locker all day waiting for him, if there was a chance he'd show up, but he wasn't supposed to know that.

As my head slowly cleared, I realized he meant had I been waiting for the custodian all day?

I took a deep breath and decided to start all over again.

"My homeroom teacher let me out early to wait for the custodian. I was just surprised to see you before the bell rang."

"Well. I sort of wanted to talk to you so I got out early too."

Calm, Maddy. Be still, my heart. This is it.

He looked away self-consciously. "You may not realize it," he began slowly, "but I'm — well, I'm sort of — see, this is very hard for me. . . ."

Hard for *him?* It's *killing* me. Go on, Adam! I've waited two months for this moment. I've been patient for two months, but I won't be able to hold out ten more seconds.

"See, the thing is, I've never — I mean, to some people this kind of thing just comes naturally, but —"

"Hey! You the kid with the busted locker?"

AARGGHH!

The custodian had arrived at last. He dropped his metal toolbox between Adam and me with a crash that resounded down the hall. Simultaneously the last bell rang.

It was all I could do to keep from screaming.

Thanks once again, oh foul-tempered God of Bad Timing.

"Did you kick it?" the custodian asked.

"Everybody kicked it!" I snapped. "The school is filled with people who kicked this locker. We call them the walking wounded."

"Sometimes you have to kick it," the custodian said stolidly. He reached into the pocket of his coveralls and pulled something out. "This should only take a minute," he said. "I got the master key. This opens all the lockers."

"Terrific," I muttered. I folded my arms.

People began streaming out of the classrooms. Most of them simply glanced at our little threesome and hurried on about their own business, but a few stopped and looked frankly curious.

The custodian inserted the key. He pulled the handle of the locker.

It didn't open.

"You must have something jammed in here," he said accusingly. "You got something jammed in here?"

"Not that I know of."

He bent down to open his toolbox. He looked at the lower part of the locker. "It looks a little dented," he said, straightening up. "You been kicking it?"

I was going to kick *him* in a minute. One of us was nuts.

A small crowd had now gathered around me, Adam, the custodian, and my broken locker.

"You could have dented it out of shape," the

custodian said. He went to work with a screwdriver and a hammer. More people gathered around to watch. I felt like an auto accident.

What was the matter with them? Why this morbid fascination with my predicament? Hadn't they ever seen a broken locker before?

Maybe they'd never seen a locker *broken* before. Which the gentleman with the toolbox was obviously trying to do.

"This dumb locker," I said to the assembled throng. "I've always had trouble with this dumb locker."

The throng nodded sympathetically, as one.

The custodian wedged the screwdriver in next to the lock and began hammering on it. The noise drew more spectators. I felt this neurotic need to explain what was going on.

Although I'd always had trouble with my locker, I was ordinarily not the type of person to cause a commotion, let alone a commotion of this proportion. I felt strangely apologetic. I started to say something — I'm not sure what — when the custodian let out a colorful stream of obscenities and dropped the hammer and the screwdriver back into his toolbox.

Everybody giggled. Except me.

I worked my way around the custodian to Adam's side.

"Do you think," I asked miserably, "he'll ever get it open?"

The custodian narrowed his eyes menacingly. "I'll get it open, girlie. No matter what you did to it."

I looked helplessly at Adam. He gave me a little smile that I'm sure was meant to be supportive, but he looked as uncomfortable as I felt in the middle of this mad scene.

"When you get it open," I said, "how do I get it open the next time? I mean, I can't call you every time I need something from my locker."

"Damn right you can't."

"Well, can you fix it?"

"How do I know? I haven't even got it open yet. I don't know what you did to it."

A moment later there was a triumphant "Aha!" and the door of my locker swung open. Spontaneous applause and cheers erupted from the audience. I had an almost irresistible impulse to take a bow, but breathed a deep sigh of relief instead.

I bent down and pulled out all my books, notebooks, everything. I nearly staggered under the weight of them, but I wasn't taking any chances.

The crowd began to thin out. The show was over. The custodian picked up his toolbox.

"What do I do now?" I asked.

"Go home," he replied. "That's what I'm going to do."

"I mean about —"

But he was already halfway down the hall.

"I'll carry some of that stuff for you," Adam said. He pulled the heaviest books from the stack and tucked them under his arm.

Would he ever continue with what he'd been about to tell me when all this happened?

"Boy, I'm sorry about this, Adam," I said. "I

111

mean, holding you up and all. I didn't realize it would take so long." Or be so ridiculous, I added silently.

"That's okay," he said. We started toward the south stairs. "But Terry must be wondering what happened to us."

I stopped short in the hallway.

"Terry?"

"Yeah. I told him I'd meet him at the car, give him a ride home."

This is it. I'm definitely going to crack. This is the final, ultimate end to my patience. I don't know what's going on here. I don't know why the blue-bird of happiness can't get off the ground, why this Love Boat can't get its anchor up, but I cannot have my emotions toyed with any longer. It is time to kiss or get off the pot.

I squared my shoulders, took a deep breath, and began. "Adam, what exactly was it that you started to say to me before all this craziness with my locker? I know you were trying to tell me something, and I'd really like to find out what it was."

He stopped at the stairwell that divided the flight of steps. He squared his shoulders too, difficult as it must have been with all the books he was carrying on his hip. I swear he took a deep breath himself before he answered, and then the words all came out in one incredible rush.

"I never went with a girl in my whole life, even though I wanted to a lot of times I never had the nerve. I liked you the first day I saw you but I never knew how to talk to girls and you didn't seem interested and so when Mary Louise started to tutor me in math I practiced on her."

He turned and practically ran down the rest of the stairs.

For a moment I was too stunned to move. I could hardly take in everything he said. He'd liked me from the first? Before I was the Brand-new Me? He'd *practiced* talking with Mary Louise, to prepare himself to talk to me?

"Adam! Adam, wait!" I ran down the stairs after him. He was standing right by the exit, looking down at the floor.

"You must think I'm a real wimp," he said dully.

"Oh, Adam, no! Oh contrairey. Wait till you hear what *I* have to tell *you!*"

Terence seemed fairly normal during the drive home. He told us that a frog can't swallow with its eyes open and that there's no white meat on a goose.

When we pulled up in front of his house, he jumped out of the car, then leaned his head inside the window of the front seat and whispered in my ear. "He's a good guy, Maddy. And I'm trying to be a good sport. How'm I doing?"

I looked into his eyes, so close to mine. After hearing the Old Terence chattering all the way from school, this took me so by surprise I just didn't know what to say.

Finally I murmured, "You're doing fine, Terence. Thank you."

He waved and walked down the drive to his house.

"That was, uh, mysterious," Adam said.

"Not really," I said shyly. "He just told me you were nice. I already knew that."

Adam blushed. "You want to — uh — go to Mc-Donald's?"

If we couldn't run off to Tahiti, that was certainly the next best thing.

Adam got us Big Macs and we sat in the car. I think both of us were trying to eat very neatly— I know I was — and wondering if it had been such a good idea to get Big Macs. I kept dabbing at my lips with a napkin after every bite and wishing I could apply more "Moist Mulberries" without Adam noticing.

"I can't believe," he said softly, "that you really liked me all along."

I'd blurted that out on the way to the car, but there hadn't been time to tell him anything else.

"I can't believe," I said, not looking at him, "that you can't believe it. Don't you know what you —" I stopped myself and took a big bite of my burger. I'd been about to mention his outrageous good looks, but caught myself just in time. Adam might be embarrassed by too graphic a description of his charms.

"When I was a kid," he said slowly, "I used to stutter. Everyone made fun of me. They imitated me. I don't know how it started — the stuttering, I mean — but it got worse and worse, until I just didn't want to talk at all. So I didn't. I mean, unless I had to in school, when I was called on. I just — sort of stayed inside myself."

"Oh, Adam." I felt like I wanted to put my arm around him and hold his head on my shoulder.

"My mother kept telling me, 'Talk slowly.' My father said I could control it if I really tried. But I couldn't and I just got to the point where I was afraid to try. I got shyer and shyer. Then my mother took me to a speech therapist and she helped me learn how to get over the stuttering, but she didn't teach me how to *talk*. I mean, you know, just talk."

He gazed out the windshield, off into the distance. His voice seemed sort of faraway. "And even after I stopped stuttering, if I got really tense or something, it sometimes came back. Not all the time, but just for that moment. And I couldn't get over the feeling that people would start laughing at me the minute I opened my mouth."

"Oh, Adam, that's awful."

"Finally I told my mother I needed help." He glanced at me quickly, waiting for my reaction.

"And?"

"She took me to a shrink." This time he looked straight at me. Was he expecting me to flinch or run screaming from the car or something?

"Did it help?"

He looked so relieved that I *hadn't* flinched or run screaming from the car that I wanted to hug him again. Later, I told myself. Hugging comes later. First comes talking.

"Well, sort of. He helped me figure out why I was hung up. But I just didn't seem to be able to get, you know, *not* hung up. I mean, so I found out why

I was shy and afraid to relate to people, but I didn't get over it. So after awhile he decided I should see a different kind of shrink. That's the one I'm seeing right now. I go twice a week, right after school." Again he seemed to wait for a reaction of shock from me. The only reaction I had was to think, "Aha! That's where he is those afternoons I don't see him at his locker!"

I crumpled up my napkin. I smiled at him. "This one *must* be helping," I said. "I mean, here we are."

He managed a little grin. "Yeah. Well, she gives me sort of homework to do. Like assignments each time I see her. And one of the things I had to do was practice talking to a girl who I didn't really care about."

"Why?" I ask curiously.

"So I wouldn't be totally wiped out if she rejected me, or if I stuttered and screwed up. The idea was to try in a situation where it didn't really matter if I failed."

"Hey, what a good idea!" I wished I'd thought of it myself two months ago.

"So when Mary Louise started to tutor me, I practiced on her. And it was hard, but we had the math to talk about anyway, so that helped."

"Adam, I have news for you. I think you were wildly successful with Mary Louise."

"What?"

"I think Mary Louise likes you."

"Don't be — oh, that's — how could —"

I could see Adam still had some work to do on his self-confidence. Don't we all, I thought.

"Anyway," he went on, shaking his head as if to

116

dismiss the thought of Mary Louise, "you were my next assignment. I mean — now I had to talk to someone who *did* matter."

"Oh, Adam."

"Am I — uh — do you think I did okay?" He looked really nervous and embarrassed. He was poking holes in the Big Mac box with his car keys.

"I think you did great," I said. "You were a lot braver than I could ever be." I could never tell him about my Seven-Day Plan. It was scary enough to admit I'd liked him since the first day I saw him, without telling him what I went through to try and make him like *me*.

"Hey, it's kind of late," he said. "I'd better get you home."

"I guess so." I looked at my books piled in the back seat. "I have a lot of work to catch up on."

He switched on the ignition. He grinned at me, almost impishly.

"Me too," he said.

117

And on the
Eighth Day ...

". . . and that's the whole story."

Sandy, Karen, and Barbara sat on the floor of my room. They'd been hanging on every word, never taking their eyes off me for an instant, except to rummage in the bottom of the potato chip bag.

"Isn't that wild? I mean, he actually liked me even before I got the new clothes and — uh — everything. He liked *me*. Plain, old me!"

"It's wild all right," Sandy said.

"Thanks a bunch."

"I just meant that you both liked each other and you were both too shy to do anything about it."

Barbara rolled her eyes. "Mmm. Just think of all the making up for lost time you'll have to do."

"We've already thought about it," I murmured.

"Did he kiss you?" Karen asked. "After he drove you home from McDonald's?"

"No," I said dreamily. "But I'm sure it's only a matter of time. He's seeing his psychologist this afternoon."

I reached for a potato chip.

"I can't wait to help him with his home-work. . . ."

About the Author

ELLEN CONFORD is the well-known award winning author of such books as *Dear Lovey Hart, I Am Desperate* and its sequel, *We Interrupt This Semester for an Important Bulletin*, as well as *If This Is Love, I'll Take Spaghetti; A Royal Pain;* and *Seven Days to a Brand-New Me*. She started writing when she was in third grade, but her first book wasn't published until much later.

Ms. Conford was born in New York City, graduated from Hofstra University, and now lives in Great Neck, Long Island, New York. Among the awards she has won for her books are the IRA/CBC Children's Choice Award, the 1983 California Young Reader Medal, the *School Library Journal* Best Book award, and a Parent's Choice Award for Literature. She is also an award winner at Scrabble and crossword puzzles.

point®

Other books you will enjoy, about real kids like you!

☐ MZ43469-1	**Arly** Robert Newton Peck		$2.95
☐ MZ40515-2	**City Light** Harry Mazer		$2.75
☐ MZ44494-8	**Enter Three Witches** Kate Gilmore		$2.95
☐ MZ40943-3	**Fallen Angels** Walter Dean Myers		$3.50
☐ MZ40847-X	**First a Dream** Maureen Daly		$3.25
☐ MZ43020-3	**Handsome as Anything** Merrill Joan Gerber		$2.95
☐ MZ43999-5	**Just a Summer Romance** Ann M. Martin		$2.75
☐ MZ44629-0	**Last Dance** Caroline B. Cooney		$2.95
☐ MZ44628-2	**Life Without Friends** Ellen Emerson White		$2.95
☐ MZ42769-5	**Losing Joe's Place** Gordon Korman		$2.95
☐ MZ43664-3	**A Pack of Lies** Geraldine McCaughrean		$2.95
☐ MZ43419-5	**Pocket Change** Kathryn Jensen		$2.95
☐ MZ43821-2	**A Royal Pain** Ellen Conford		$2.95
☐ MZ44429-0	**A Semester in the Life of a Garbage Bag** Gordon Korman		$2.95
☐ MZ43867-0	**Son of Interflux** Gordon Korman		$2.95
☐ MZ43971-5	**The Stepfather Game** Norah McClintock		$2.95
☐ MZ41513-1	**The Tricksters** Margaret Mahy		$2.95
☐ MZ43638-4	**Up Country** Alden R. Carter		$2.95

Watch for new titles coming soon!
Available wherever you buy books, or use this order form.

Scholastic Inc., P.O. Box 7502, 2931 E. McCarty Street, Jefferson City, MO 65102

Please send me the books I have checked above. I am enclosing $ _____
Please add $2.00 to cover shipping and handling. Send check or money order - no cash or C.O.D's please.

Name _____

Address _____

City _____ State/Zip _____

Please allow four to six weeks for delivery. Offer good in U.S.A. only. Sorry, mail orders are not available to residents of Canada. Prices subject to changes.

PNT891

point® **THRILLERS**

R.L. Stine
- ☐ MC44236-8 The Baby-sitter $3.50
- ☐ MC44332-1 The Baby-sitter II $3.50
- ☐ MC45386-6 Beach House $3.25
- ☐ MC43278-8 Beach Party $3.50
- ☐ MC43125-0 Blind Date $3.50
- ☐ MC43279-6 The Boyfriend $3.50
- ☐ MC44333-X The Girlfriend $3.50
- ☐ MC45385-8 Hit and Run $3.25
- ☐ MC46100-1 The Hitchhiker $3.50
- ☐ MC43280-X The Snowman $3.50
- ☐ MC43139-0 Twisted $3.50

Caroline B. Cooney
- ☐ MC44316-X The Cheerleader $3.25
- ☐ MC41641-3 The Fire $3.25
- ☐ MC43806-9 The Fog $3.25
- ☐ MC45681-4 Freeze Tag $3.25
- ☐ MC45402-1 The Perfume $3.25
- ☐ MC44884-6 The Return of the Vampire $2.95
- ☐ MC41640-5 The Snow $3.25
- ☐ MC45682-2 The Vampire's Promise $3.50

Diane Hoh
- ☐ MC44330-5 The Accident $3.25
- ☐ MC45401-3 The Fever $3.25
- ☐ MC43050-5 Funhouse $3.25
- ☐ MC44904-4 The Invitation $3.50
- ☐ MC45640-7 The Train (9/92) $3.25

Sinclair Smith
- ☐ MC45063-8 The Waitress $2.95

Christopher Pike
- ☐ MC43014-9 Slumber Party $3.50
- ☐ MC44256-2 Weekend $3.50

A. Bates
- ☐ MC45829-9 The Dead Game $3.25
- ☐ MC43291-5 Final Exam $3.25
- ☐ MC44582-0 Mother's Helper $3.50
- ☐ MC44238-4 Party Line $3.25

D.E. Athkins
- ☐ MC45246-0 Mirror, Mirror $3.25
- ☐ MC45349-1 The Ripper $3.25
- ☐ MC44941-9 Sister Dearest $2.95

Carol Ellis
- ☐ MC44768-8 My Secret Admirer $3.25
- ☐ MC46044-7 The Stepdaughter $3.25
- ☐ MC44916-8 The Window $2.95

Richie Tankersley Cusick
- ☐ MC43115-3 April Fools $3.25
- ☐ MC43203-6 The Lifeguard $3.25
- ☐ MC43114-5 Teacher's Pet $3.25
- ☐ MC44235-X Trick or Treat $3.25

Lael Littke
- ☐ MC44237-6 Prom Dress $3.25

Edited by T. Pines
- ☐ MC45256-8 Thirteen $3.50